A Note to Reade

Though Janie's story is fictional, her experience represents that of many African-Americans following the Civil War.

In 1861, the United States of America were anything but united. Verbal battles between the states erupted into a bloody, all-out war. Fought on America's own soil, Northerner against Southerner, this "War Between the States" lasted from 1861 until 1865.

Many things were disputed in the war, but the most compelling issue was the existence of slavery in America. Much of young America was built by slave labor, and this was especially true in the Southern states. Early Southern plantations provided a wonderful life for wealthy whites, but this came from the unpaid labor of their black slaves who were either kidnapped from their homes in Africa and transported across the Atlantic Ocean or born into slavery to previous generations of captives.

Fortunately, many Americans believed that no one had the right to own other human beings. The Emancipation Proclamation was issued by President Abraham Lincoln in 1862 and went into effect on New Year's Day in 1863. This decree was to free Southern slaves, though it was largely ignored until the war was over. (Northern slaves were freed in 1865 by the Thirteenth Amendment.)

In the story that follows, you'll meet young Janie, a fictitious, freed Southern slave. It's two years after the end of the Civil War. Like many former slaves, Janie does not know where her family members are—they were separated and sold to different owners before the war began. And like many former slaves with their first taste of freedom, she finds a whole new world opening to her.

SISTERS IN TIME

Janie's
Freedom

AFRICAN-AMERICANS IN THE
AFTERMATH OF THE CIVIL WAR

CALLIE SMITH GRANT

BARBOUR
PUBLISHING

Janie's
Freedom

Cover design by Lookout Design Group, Inc.

Published by Barbour Publishing, Inc., P.O. Box 719, Uhrichsville, Ohio 44683
www.barbourbooks.com

Our mission is to publish and distribute inspirational products offering exceptional value and biblical encouragement to the masses.

 Member of the
Evangelical Christian
Publishers Association

Printed in the United States of America.

5 4 3 2 1

CONTENTS

CHAPTER 1

Rubyhill

"Janie! Janie!" Aleta ran down the main path of the slave quarters. "Come quick! There's a carriage with horses! Something's happening!"

Eleven-year-old Janie stopped sweeping the dirt in front of the cabin she shared with old Aunty Mil. It was a lovely September morning at Rubyhill Plantation, and Janie had been making pretty patterns in the dirt with the broom. Inside the one-room cabin, Aunty Mil warmed herself by a fire. Janie propped the straw broom against the log wall of the cabin and trotted up the knoll toward seventeen-year-old Aleta.

Aleta was Janie's friend, even though they were not the same age. The older girl had taken Janie under her wing in the plantation kitchen when Janie first arrived at Rubyhill six years ago. Aleta acted like a big sister to Janie—even called her "little sis" sometimes—and that was fine. While Janie wore her hair in braids, Aleta covered her own hair with a bright scarf tied in back like a grown woman.

"Come on, Janie," Aleta said. "You got to see this." She grabbed Janie's hand and pulled her the rest of the way up the knoll, taking them both out of the quarters.

The two ran to the front of the Rubyhill Plantation's mansion, the place everyone called the Big House. There in the weedy horseshoe drive stood a fine carriage drawn by a handsome pair of matching gray horses. Janie had not seen such well-fed creatures in a long time, not since the war started and the master and his son rode off to fight in it. Even the Yankee soldiers who came through Georgia two years before had not ridden such fine horses.

She shifted her attention to the carriage itself. It was made of wood and shining leather. The wheels were straight, and their black paint showed through the red road dust. The driver, a white man, sat ramrod-straight, buggy whip in hand, eyes straight ahead. He looked uncomfortable, maybe from all the sudden attention he was receiving from the former slaves of Rubyhill. Janie noticed that he also looked quite well fed. She wondered where he was getting food.

Most of Rubyhill's twenty former slaves joined Janie and Aleta in the front yard, standing at a slight distance from the horse and carriage. It was some sight to see, these pretty horses and their stout white driver sitting in the sun in the middle of the fire-scorched front yard. Janie and Aleta whispered to each other, but the others stayed silent and alert.

After nearly a quarter hour, the former slaves heard a noise behind them. Turning almost as one, they watched two men gently lead Miz Laura down what was left of the broken-down veranda stairs. Miz Laura was the mistress at Rubyhill, and she looked thin and old beyond her years. She wore a too-large, wrinkled black dress and a black straw hat that tied under her chin. Her shabbily gloved hands gripped the arms of the men flanking her as she slowly moved toward the carriage. *What's happening here?* Janie wondered, but she kept silent.

With some difficulty, Miz Laura climbed into the carriage,

helped by the men, who then swung up behind her. She placed a hand on the driver's shoulder. "Wait, please," she said in a soft voice. She turned in her seat to the crowd of freed slaves.

She took her time looking each person in the eyes, one by one. The strangeness of this hit them all; never had Miz Laura—nor any other white person—ever sought direct eye contact with the slaves. The group stood uncomfortably silent, but many, including Janie, returned her gaze.

The woman began to speak in a weary voice. "These men are my cousins from Pennsylvania. That is where I'm from." She paused and looked off in the distance for a moment. "It's become painfully clear that my husband and my son will not be returning to Rubyhill ever again. My family has sent for me, and as I'm certain you can understand, I've decided to return home with them." She paused again and sighed. "I want to thank you good people. You kept me from starving. I do not know how you did it. I even wonder why you did it. But I greatly appreciate it."

Miz Laura looked around her at the Big House, with its broken front pillars, collapsed roof, and blackened walls. She gazed at the stumps of the once-mighty oaks that had lined the long drive, the broken stone walls of the burned-out formal gardens, the acres of overgrown fields, no longer blackened by the fire set by the Yankees but also no longer green with planting.

"I ask your forgiveness," she said suddenly. "I should have insisted my husband give you a better life while I could. I was wrong, and I regret it now, every moment of every day." She stared at her gloved hands for a moment, then looked at the small crowd again. "Stay at Rubyhill as long as you like. Take whatever you can use from the house or from anywhere else on this land. My men won't be coming back. Neither will I. May God bless you all and keep you safe."

Miz Laura leaned back and placed one hand over her eyes. As one of the cousins draped a carriage blanket over Miz Laura's lap, Aleta called out a blessing to the white woman. The others murmured good-byes or remained silent as the driver flicked his buggy whip and the carriage rolled down the drive in a rosy cloud of Georgia dust.

The community of former slaves dispersed thoughtfully. Janie and Aleta waited until they could no longer see the carriage, then they walked quietly back to the slave quarters together. Finally Janie said, "What's it mean, Aleta? Miz Laura's never comin' back?"

"Looks like it," replied Aleta.

As they approached Janie's cabin, Aunty Mil's reedy voice came from the door. "What's going on, Janie-bird?"

Aleta waved to Janie and headed back to the yard. Janie waved back and ducked into the cabin. "Miz Laura's cousins come got her. They's goin' north."

"Mm-mm." This was Aunty Mil's response to many things in life. Arthritic and blind with age, she spent her days rocking in a broken chair, trying to keep her old body warm.

The rocker had come from the Big House. Janie had seen the Yankee General Sherman and his soldiers throw it through a glass window when they came through Rubyhill on their path of destruction. The chair had lost an arm and the tip of a runner in the process, but it still rocked. And it had a nice, thick, embroidered seat cushion.

Janie had watched it get rained on in the yard. Then it dried out. When a rainstorm approached again, she had asked the older slaves if she could take the chair to Aunty Mil. The elders had said yes. Janie had picked the glass out of the cushion; then she dragged the chair to the quarters all by herself. At the time, it had been almost bigger than she was. Aunty Mil liked the chair and now rarely left it.

"Wanna sit in the sun, Aunty Mil?"

"Yes, baby girl. Thank you so much."

Janie helped the old woman up, dragged the chair to the dirt path outside the cabin, and placed it square in the sun. Aunty Mil hobbled out and sank onto the now-worn cushion. Janie noticed the old woman's face was bathed in sweat.

"You all right, Aunty?"

"Yes. That fire in there kinda hot all of a sudden is all." Blindness had turned Aunty Mil's eyes light blue. Now she closed them and leaned back. "Ooh, that's a good breeze." She rocked a moment. "Now tell Aunty Mil all about what happened up there."

Janie told the old woman about the handsome carriage and matched gray horses and Miz Laura's speech. "Mm-mm," the old woman responded. "Change in the air." She was suddenly fast asleep. Janie noticed that was happening a lot lately.

Janie grabbed the broom and quickly finished sweeping the yard, swirling patterns in the dirt and thinking about what had just happened. Then she went about her daily task of finding food that Aunty Mil could eat without having to chew, since the old woman was missing many of her teeth. Janie had exhausted most of the plantation's possible stashing places, but she still managed to find some she hadn't remembered before.

And although she couldn't remember every place she had hidden food, Janie remembered the rest of the events of two years ago as if they had happened yesterday. That day was a milestone in her life, like the day her father was sold to the chain gang and the day a year later when little Janie was sold away from her mother and brought here to Rubyhill. The day General Sherman and his soldiers came to Rubyhill marked a line in the Georgia clay; there was life before the Yankees and life after the Yankees. And nothing nowadays was anything like it had been before.

Back then, a runner came panting into the slave quarters one day. He was from Bailey Meadows, a plantation several miles away, and he'd been sent to warn Miz Laura and the others that the Yankees were about thirty miles down the road and headed this way. The word was that they were stealing what they could and destroying anything else in their path.

Miz Laura already had her many valuable things buried in the fields and gardens in case the Yankees might come to Rubyhill. Now the slaves figured they had a couple days to take care of what really mattered, and they got to work.

First they slaughtered and cooked two pigs for the next couple days' food. Then they scattered the other pigs into the fields and woods. They found hiding places for hams and wheels of cheese.

Miz Laura had not given thought to the canned goods and other root-cellar items, but the slaves did. They sent the children to find places in the forest and fields to hide anything small and edible. For three days and two nights, Janie and the other child slaves carted glass jars of fruits, vegetables, and preserves out of the cellar and hid them in the nearby woods. They buried potatoes, carrots, and turnips in the dirt all over the fields. Whatever eggs the hens laid were boiled; after they cooled, the children covered the eggs in mud and tucked them into the slave-cabin fireplaces.

Then they chased the hens into the woods.

It was late on the third day when the soldiers arrived. Indeed, they took any food they could find in the smokehouse and kitchen. They took the milking cows and whatever goats, sheep, pigs, and chickens had made their way back to the barnyards. There were no horses left at Rubyhill—they'd already been taken by Confederate soldiers for the war effort.

Now Sherman's men took anything they considered valuable from the house—big, thick rugs, paintings, even stacks of china dishes—and then they set fire to the house, the barns, and the stables, the fields, and every tree they could torch, even the peach trees. The slaves were especially surprised by that part.

In the middle of the screaming and yelling, the Yankee general himself shouted the announcement that the slaves were free. "Every bit as free as I am," he emphasized. Then the troops moved east through the pungent black smoke, singing as they marched. They had not touched the slave quarters.

A few pigs and chickens wandered back during the next week or so. Some hams and cheeses had escaped detection, and potatoes buried in the burned fields tasted nicely roasted when they were dug up. The Yankees had avoided the plantation's beehives, so there was honey.

Soon enough, however, they ate all the hidden food that was easy to find. Except for a few chickens, the remaining livestock had to be killed for meat. The plantation's inhabitants lived off whatever forest edibles they could find and whatever fish and game they could rustle up, vegetables they could grow, eggs from the laying hens, and any food the children found from their many hiding places. It was plenty of work just keeping everyone fed.

Today, Janie thought she remembered where she had buried a jar of preserves, and she set out with a large spoon for digging. After digging in an area around a patch of rhubarb gone to seed, she did indeed find a glass jar of peach preserves. She cleaned it off with her apron, then carefully cradled it to take back to Aunty Mil, eager to give her something sweet and soft.

On the way, she saw several of the former slaves gathered around the pump. Janie spied Aleta and headed for her side. Seventeen-year-old Blue, a well-liked young man, was saying to the others, "I believe it's time to go in the Big House and see if there's somethin' we can use."

An elder shook his head. "Miz Laura may think nobody comin' back here, but sooner or later, somebody be back to claim this land, burned or not."

After a long pause, Aleta spoke up. "Well, for now, I think Blue's right. We ought to find what we can use around here. Miz Laura said we could—we all heard her. I say let's go to the Big House."

The Big House cook shook her head. "I want nothin' to do with going in there. That house is haunted."

Blue looked at her and laughed. "You been goin' in there for years. Why you say it's haunted now?"

"Miz Laura was there then. It don't feel right going in there now. Too much misery."

"Come on, Cookie," said Aleta. "Miz Laura gave us her blessing. You heard her. Let's you and me go in there together and see what we find. No need to fear an empty house. It's just empty." Aleta linked arms with the heavyset cook and pulled her along to the back door of the house. "Let's go find us something good, Cookie."

Janie hurried back to her cabin with the preserves and woke up Aunty Mil. "I found something soft for you, Aunty," she said as she pried open the jar.

The old woman dipped a finger in and tasted the peachy sweetness. "Ooh, child, you done it now," she cackled. "Tastes that good."

"I'll be right back, Aunty," said Janie. "People going in the Big House like Miz Laura said we could. I'll see if I can find something else for you to eat." She handed a spoon to Aunty Mil.

"I thank you, Janie-bird." Aunty Mil stopped dipping her finger into the preserves and began spooning little bites, savoring the syrupy fruit. "I thank you for many things, baby girl."

Janie laughed and trotted through the quarters again. A slight girl but with strong legs and arms, Janie was always running or dancing about, and she was known as a good worker. She remembered a time when they weren't always trying to find food, but it seemed like that's all they did now. And Janie was always hungry.

Maybe there would be some surprises in the Big House. Maybe there was even food still hidden somewhere in there.

Janie hurried up to the Big House.

CHAPTER 2

Inside the Big House

Janie, Aleta, and Blue stood inside what was left of the main entrance hall of Rubyhill's Big House and looked up the charred spiral staircase to the hole in the roof. They had entered with the cook through the side door, and now the three young people stood in this front hallway. Miz Laura had called it the foyer.

It felt strange to Janie to be inside the Big House. In the past two years, Miz Laura had not moved much of anything since the day the Yankees destroyed so much of it. She'd ordered the others to leave things as they were for some unexplained reason. It was a mess.

"Dunno how that woman stayed in her right mind living like this," muttered Aleta.

"Seems she lost her right mind," offered Blue.

Aleta shrugged. "Sounded right in her mind to me when she left. Sounded sad is all."

Janie gazed around the foyer, which was a big room in itself. She vividly remembered the parties here before the war and how she'd peek in from the dining room. It was something to see, all those ladies in their great big hoopskirts, milling about, holding on to the arms of tall, well-dressed gentlemen. They had all fit in here just fine with plenty of room to spare.

Now this once grand entrance area was dark and dingy. The

door to the front veranda was tied shut with baling twine. Scattered around the room were broken urns and glass from window panes and once-beloved possessions, sagging drapes, slashed paintings of previous Rubyhill inhabitants, and general filth. It plainly showed the two years of neglect that had followed the fire.

"Maybe we can use them drapes," Aleta remarked. She was a good seamstress. "I could make blankets out of 'em."

Janie hesitantly slid open the pocket doors to the parlor. Since the upstairs fire, this was where Miz Laura had been living, and she hadn't left the room much at all. One of the former slaves had continued to help her, cooking and doing her laundry. This was done for her strictly out of kindness, since slavery was over.

At any rate, it appeared that Miz Laura had been sleeping in this room on a once-fine couch, its velvet ripped open by a Yankee's sword. She'd left her blankets and bedclothes strewn around. Janie tiptoed over to them. She shook them out and set them aside to be used by the community of former slaves.

"I'm going upstairs," she heard Blue announce from the foyer.

"You crazy?" Aleta fussed. "Half the stairs is burned out."

Blue laughed. Janie hurried to the hallway and watched as he headed up to the charred area. Always nimble on his feet, Blue climbed and pulled himself from solid point to solid point and got to the upstairs balcony. Janie thought he looked like a cat climbing a tree.

Blue disappeared into the first bedroom. "Soldiers took this room apart, that's for sure!" he yelled from inside.

"Hey, Blue!" Aleta called up. "See if they went into the middle rooms where the clothes were! No windows on those, so it's gonna be dark in there!"

After a few moments, Blue showed up at the banister. "Nobody touched those rooms, Aleta. Must'a been too busy ripping apart everything else, but those rooms—the doors ain't even open. Most of the rooms burned through the roof, though."

"I want to go up there," said Janie.

"No, little sis," said Aleta. "Too dangerous."

Blue laughed. "For her? She's surefooted as a goat, and she don't weigh enough to make anything collapse. Come on up, girl. Follow what I tell you."

Janie listened to Blue and took every step and handhold he instructed her to take until she had made her way up to the second floor. "Wanna come up?" she called down to Aleta.

The older girl shook her head. "I'll go through what's down here. Let me know what you find."

Janie had never been upstairs in all her time at Rubyhill. She'd never climbed the circular staircase when it was intact. The kitchen was detached from the house, as were most plantation kitchens, partly because of the intense southern heat and partly as a safety precaution in case a cooking fire surged out of control. Because Janie was a kitchen worker, the only indoor rooms she'd been in were the pantry and the dining room.

The five upstairs bedrooms had doors off a U-shaped balcony that looked over the foyer downstairs. All the bedrooms had extensive damage from smashing, slashing, and fire, as well as from rain, since most of the roof had burned out.

Just as Aleta said, some of the bedrooms were connected by dressing rooms that ran between them. The soldiers had entered bedrooms by way of the hallway doors and, in their haste, hadn't disturbed the dressing rooms.

Blue and Janie discovered that the dressing room in what had been Miz Laura's bedroom was untouched by the fire. There was a smoky smell, but flames had not reached that small part of the roof. It was dark in there, but even in the dim light, they could see some clothes and wardrobe drawers.

Blue left Janie in Miz Laura's bedroom and ran to find candles. Janie sank down on her haunches and looked around, then up at the gaping hole in the roof. She could see straight up at the sky through the burned-out part. So blue, and not a cloud in it. *Hard to believe anything bad happened here when you look up high,* she thought. A family of goldfinches had built nests in the charred boards, and the birds were noisy and upset over Janie's intrusion. She spoke gently to the largest bird. "Don't worry, little momma, we won't be here long."

Momma. Janie had a quick vision of her mother back at Shannon Oaks, smiling at her in the rosy light of the cabin fire. She had strong memories of Momma stroking her head and singing songs about Jesus to her. Before Poppa was taken away on the chain gang, Momma used to laugh a lot. But nobody knew where Poppa had been taken. There wasn't much laughter after that day.

Janie'd last seen Momma at Shannon Oaks Plantation, the very place where Janie had been born on Christmas Day eleven years ago. Few slaves knew their birthdays. But since Christmas Day was the one day every year slaves did not have to work, it was easy to remember that day was Janie's birthday.

She sometimes wondered about going to find Momma, but Janie had never been away from Rubyhill since the day she was brought here six years ago as a small child. She had no idea how to get to Shannon Oaks. She wasn't even sure how far away it was.

Of course, Janie knew north from south and east from west like every other country child. But she really didn't have a clear idea as to where she lived in relation to the rest of the world. Rubyhill itself was her world.

The most disturbing thing, though, was that there was no telling where Momma might be now. Poppa was sold south the year before little Janie was sold to Rubyhill, and since then, Momma could have been sold, too. Besides, if Momma were still around, wouldn't she come find Janie?

This was the question that often nudged its way into Janie's young heart. It was a question that had left her hopeful after the soldiers told them they were free. But as time went on, she found that question made her heart ache. She didn't think she could go searching for Momma, but she sure wished Momma would search for her. If she could.

Blue crashed his way back into the room, holding a big torch and a couple of squat candles.

"How you get up them stairs with that fire?" Janie asked.

"Wasn't easy, girl, but here I am." He squatted down and handed Janie the candles. After lighting both candles, he walked to a smashed-out window and called down to the yard. "Ready, Nathan, Lucy?" Ten-year-old Nathan and his twin sister, Lucy, were good friends of Janie. They stood below the window, a waterlogged blanket stretched between them. Blue tossed the lighted torch out the window, watched as Nathan and Lucy caught and doused the torch with the blanket, and then turned back to Janie.

Blue took one lighted candle from her and approached the dressing room. "Come on, girl. Let's see what we got in here."

Shannon Oaks Plantation, Georgia

Forty miles away at Shannon Oaks Plantation, a former slave named Anna picked her final ear of corn for the day. She and the others dumped each of their heavy canvas bags full of corn into piles at the end of each row. There would be plenty to eat for a while.

The former slaves of Shannon Oaks were undoubtedly eating better than many other Georgians. Food wasn't necessarily plentiful, but at least Shannon Oaks had not been in the direct path of Sherman and his men. Not all had been lost that day in Georgia.

And Anna had seen plenty of loss over the past few years. Her young husband had been chained up and taken from her before the war. One year later, her brown-eyed little girl was sold and taken away. Anna had been beside herself with grief.

But she held on. Every day Anna hoped and prayed the three of them would be together again. She didn't know where they were. George could be anywhere south of Shannon Oaks. Maybe Mississippi, she'd heard. And little Janie—really named Georgeanna after both her parents—was last known to be at a plantation called Rubyhill.

Anna sometimes thought about striking out for that place called Rubyhill. Only one thing held her back.

The day George was chained onto the chain gang and led down the long drive at Shannon Oaks, Anna had run alongside him, frantic. It was horrible to see her strong, handsome husband in chains. Anna had wept openly.

"Don't you cry, woman!" George called to her. His eyes flashed in a mix of anger, fear, and love. "You stay strong. You stay strong for Janie." He had held Anna's gaze with his own as he was pulled away, then said the words she would not forget: "I'll come back and get you. I'll come back."

Anna was holding him to it. The war had been over for almost two years now. When would George come back? And when could they go find their little girl?

Anna slipped two ears of corn into her apron pocket to roast later on. She kept her strength up by eating even when she'd rather do anything but eat. Because no matter where George had ended up, if he said he was coming back, he'd be back.

If he was still alive, that is.

CHAPTER 3

The Leather Box

In spite of the general smokiness, a sweet waft of cedar met Janie when she and Blue opened the wardrobe doors. They both worked quickly by candlelight, pulling out all the clothing they could find, first in one room and then in all the upstairs dressing rooms.

There were shirts and pants, dresses, skirts, blouses, night-gowns, robes, warm coats, lightweight jackets, and the real prize: shoes and boots. *Them Yankees were in some hurry to miss all this,* Janie thought. A few woolen items had started to get moth-eaten, but the cedar walls had protected most of them.

Piece by piece, Janie and Blue pulled clothing out of the wardrobes and hauled everything to an open window. There they dropped the items to the eager hands of former slaves who had gathered below.

On plantations, the only clothes slaves had were the ones on their backs, and technically they didn't even own those. Every year each person was issued one outfit of clothing and one blanket. Shoes were scarce even in better times, and it was not unusual to go barefoot all year long.

Since midway through the war, however, no clothing or blankets had been issued at Rubyhill. Everyone's clothing was looking threadbare. There hadn't been enough wool for winter for a couple of years, and even in Georgia, winters could be chilly. Janie recalled waking up to a dusting of snow on the ground once in a while.

At least now, she knew Rubyhill's ex-slaves would manage to stay dressed and warm for a long time with all these fine garments.

Eventually, Janie and Blue carefully made their way back down the burned staircase. The sun was lowering, and it was starting to give everything indoors an eerie shadow. Janie was eager to get out of this dark house and into the fresh air. She was also eager to join the other members of the community in sorting through the huge piles of clothes now at their disposal.

"Be sure Janie gets something nice," Janie heard Aleta reminding them. "She worked hard hunting and hauling for y'all."

Janie appreciated Aleta's big-sister ways. She was a little bossy, but nobody minded, simply because Aleta had the interests of them all at heart. She was wise beyond her seventeen years, and everyone saw it.

"Come over here, Janie," Aleta said.

Janie hurried to where Aleta rummaged through the huge piles of clothing. She pulled out a lovely calico-print dress and held it lengthwise in front of Janie. Aleta's experienced eye took in all of Janie's slender body. "Miz Laura's bigger than you, but not so much. I can cut this down some."

Aleta looked back at the pile. "Master and his son sure had a lot of clothes for menfolk. Most everybody should be able to find a coat here."

Janie began rummaging. She found a pair of warm slippers that would fit Aunty Mil. Then she pulled out a thick jacket that had belonged to the master's son, but on Janie it was a full-length coat. She rolled the sleeves up, over and over. Aleta looked over at her and laughed. "I'll trim that down, too, but you don't need that right away. We got a little time before cold sets in."

Janie rummaged until she found a pair of thick socks that would help Aunty's cold feet. Then she found some shoes that she could wear herself and a jacket that would fit Aunty Mil.

Janie straightened up and looked around. The rose trellises lay in pieces in bunches of weeds, never having been cleaned up. The many roses and other flowering bushes were long gone.

Only now did Janie notice a few of the other former slaves pulling at the weeds and digging with big spoons in and around the old flowerbeds. Both Nathan and Lucy sat cross-legged, digging at the ground in front of them with cooking spoons.

Valuables had been buried very well in the gardens, and plants were put in the ground right over them. The Yankees hadn't found a thing there, not that they didn't try. But back when Miz Laura was still giving orders, she had said to leave that sort of thing buried because there might be stray thieves roaming the countryside. So today was the first digging anyone had done in the gardens.

"Find anything?" Janie called out to Nathan and Lucy.

"Nah, not yet," Nathan replied. Lucy shook her head.

Old Joe, one of the elders, called out, "I got me something here." He pulled a dirt-covered box up out of the ground and set it in front of him. He squatted back on his haunches and brushed the dirt off the box. "This here box is made of leather," he commented. "I seen it before." He pried the box open, then gave a long, low whistle.

Janie sidled next to Old Joe and looked over his shoulder. The box, which was about the size of four loaves of bread laid out side by side, was full of paper money.

"Rebel cash," remarked Blue. "Ain't worth a thing no more."

"Rebel cash ain't worth a thing, all right," said Old Joe with a chuckle. "But this here works just fine."

Everyone became silent. Finally Aleta spoke. "What are you saying, Old Joe?"

"Only thing rebel money's good for is kindling, true enough. I'm saying this here's Yankee money. This here money works fine."

Blue squatted down next to Old Joe. Blue reached in the box and touched the money, then pulled his hand back as if he'd touched something hot. "How you know that?" he asked.

Old Joe stood, stretched, and shook his head. "You young'uns don't think I got a mind for nothin'. What you think I did all them years with Master?"

Nobody answered. Old Joe snorted. "I kept the books."

Still nobody responded until Nathan said, "You mean you can read?"

Janie was stunned by that possibility. It had been illegal to teach slaves to read, and as far as she knew, nobody among them had ever learned.

"No, boy, not them kinda books. I can't read any better'n you, son," said Old Joe. "But Master made sure I could figure. He taught me numbers so's I could keep the books for taking crops in and make sure he didn't get cheated at the mills."

Old Joe rubbed the small of his back. "So I know numbers. And I know what money looks like. I know when it turned rebel cash, what that looked like, too. And I heard talk about this here Yankee money. Master told Miz Laura to hide it in case she need it to go north some day. We all buried this two years ago, not knowing what we buried."

"Well, why didn't she have us dig it back up?" asked Blue.

Old Joe shrugged. "She never was right in the head after them Yankees—you know that."

The cook spoke up. "Nobody hurts for money in Miz Laura's family, even after all this war. You saw them horses, that big white man driver. Miz Laura probably forgot all about this money in the ground."

"Maybe she just wanted to get out of here as fast as she could," offered Aleta.

Janie stared at the box of money. She'd never had an occasion to see money except when the chain gang had come through to buy slaves, and even then it was never a box of money. Those memories were too hurtful to think about, anyway.

"How much you figure is there, Old Joe?" Janie asked.

"A whole lot. I can tell you that much," he said.

"Us black folks use that money 'round here, white folks gonna think we stole it," Blue groused.

Old Joe looked at Blue for a long moment. Then he looked around at the others. The lowering sun turned his skin a golden hue, it seemed to Janie, just like the fine oak furniture she used to polish in the Big House dining room.

"You most likely right on that part," Old Joe said. "We can use some of it now and then, here and there. But the rest, you gonna take, boy. You goin' north."

For once Blue was speechless, and so was everyone else. It was little Janie who finally spoke up. "What you mean, Old Joe?"

Old Joe placed his old dry hand on Janie's head. "I mean this, child. . .you young'uns here got to go north. There's nothing down here for you. You got to get out of here, get work, learn to read and write. Nobody here can teach you that."

Janie felt sick to her stomach at the thought of anyone going anywhere. She'd lived on Rubyhill for more than half her life. For better or worse, Rubyhill was home, and these people had become her family. "But. . .why?" she stammered.

Old Joe tugged lightly on one of Janie's braids. " 'Cause that's how it's got to be, child." He looked out beyond the gardens. "I been places y'all never been. I been north, even. Master trusted me to go with him—everybody knows that. I woulda run, but I couldn't leave my wife and babies down here on their own, and Master knew it. I meant to fly out of here some day and take them north with me, but when my wife took sick. . .my babies gone. . .that war. . ."

Old Joe turned and looked around the silent group. "Any old ones want to go, that's fine, but I'm past that now. My woman's dead, my girls sold off." He paused. "I'm saying you young'uns got to have a chance. As long as you stay here, maybe you know in your mind you're free, but not in your heart. Never in your heart. You'll still think like a Georgia slave. Rubyhill still a plantation owned by white folks." He snorted and shook his head. "Crazy white folks, at that."

Janie noticed for the first time that Old Joe was getting filmy blue eyes just like Aunty Mil.

Blue finally recovered from being dumbfounded. "Old Joe, I ain't never thought about these things."

"Well, boy, time you did. 'Cause you the one gonna lead 'em north."

Blue's mouth dropped open again. "But where would we go?"

Old Joe looked off in the distance for a moment. "I been thinkin' 'bout Chicago. Way up north and mighty cold, but I hear tell there's work for everybody there, black or white. Big cold city. Sits on water big as a ocean—Lake Michigan. That lake don't belong to nobody, so's you can fish on it plenty and nobody'll bother you."

Old Joe went silent. Then he looked back at Blue. "I been there, son, plenty times. I can tell you how to get there." With that, Old Joe picked up the box of money and walked back to the quarters.

It took a long moment for the others to go back to work. Janie stood thoughtfully, worried about the changes that seemed to be happening no matter how she felt about them.

The cook snapped her out of her reverie. "Come here and help—I just found the silver."

The group moved over to circle around Cookie. Everyone pulled silver dishes and cups wrapped in newspaper and cloth out of the ground. They worked quickly, piling all the pieces on top of one of the flowerbeds. "We can sell this," the cook said. "Or trade it. Maybe we can get flour and rice and such."

Janie started when Nathan tapped her on the shoulder. "I found this, Janie," he said. "Want it?" He held out a cross on a long silver chain.

Janie took the cross. She placed it in the palm of her hand and looked it over while Nathan moved back to his digging. The heavy cross was made of pewter. There was writing on the back of it but, of course, Janie couldn't read it. She placed the chain around her neck, and the pewter cross dangled halfway down her chest. She didn't want the cross to get snagged on anything as she worked, so she tucked it inside her dress. She made her way over to Nathan and beamed at him. "Thanks, Nathan."

Nathan grinned, and he and Janie both went back to digging.

As dusk fell, Janie gathered her haul of clothing and took it back to the cabin.

Aunty Mil was grateful for the slippers, which Janie put on her feet for her. "Older I get, seems the less my blood gets down to my feet," Aunty Mil said.

As for Janie, the day had been so full of excitement that she had trouble staying awake while she told Aunty Mil about it. Finally the old woman chuckled and told Janie to go to bed. "Let's talk in the morning, child."

Janie collapsed on her pallet next to the fire. Just before she fell asleep, she fingered the pewter cross. The thought came to her, *If you go north and learn to read, you'll know what it says on this cross.* Then she fell sound asleep.

That night, Janie dreamed she was eating a big jar of succotash. How good it tasted! When she woke up, she could still taste it. Only then did she remember that she'd buried that very thing two years ago under a floorboard of the detached kitchen.

Later she found it was right where she'd hidden it.

CHAPTER 4

"I Got to Go"

Janie stirred cornmeal mush and canned peaches around in the big black pot over the cabin fire. Aunty Mil rocked steadily in her chair, humming and moaning. Moaning was something Aunty Mil did sometimes when she prayed or thought about the past. It was just a way she had of expressing herself, and Janie had gotten used to it.

"Aunty Mil, you hungry now? I'll spoon this up if you're ready."

"Yes, Janie-bird, I'm ready."

Janie scooped the thick, sweet concoction with a big ladle Cookie had given her from the Big House kitchen. The mush dropped into a chipped bowl with a pleasant-sounding *splat*. Janie lifted Aunty Mil's hand so she could feel how warm the bowl was. Then she steered a spoon into the woman's other hand.

Aunty Mil thanked Janie and placed the bowl securely in her lap. She automatically said the meal's blessing, just as she did for all meals.

"Lord in Heaven, we thank You for this food," Aunty Mil prayed. "Keep my Janie safe and sound in all her ways. I pray for traveling mercies for her and the others on their journey north. Amen."

Aunty Mil took a bite and made an appreciative noise.

But Janie sat silently. The prayer had unsettled her. She had not yet spoken to Aunty Mil about that part of yesterday's events. Janie had gone to sleep quickly last night, and this morning she had run out of the cabin very early. How did Aunty Mil know about all that talk from yesterday? And why did she pray that way? Janie wasn't planning on going anywhere.

Janie scooped out a portion of syrupy mush and squatted down to eat. But her stomach had twisted into a knot. She put her bowl down and watched Aunty Mil instead.

The old woman had a half smile on her face as she ate her soft food. She'd had to refuse the succotash Janie found earlier, because the corn really needed to be chewed. But the old woman was very pleased with this soft meal, and she ate it happily.

"Aunty," Janie finally blurted out, "how you know people's fixin' to leave Rubyhill?"

Without missing a bite, the old woman chuckled and said, "Don't you know this place got no secrets? Ain't nothing strange about that, baby. Word just gets around—that's all."

Janie sat down on the cabin's dirt floor. "But I ain't going nowhere, Aunty. Not without you."

"Yes, you are, child," Aunty Mil said gently.

"Why you say that?" Janie was feeling even more unsettled.

" 'Cause it's your time, baby. It's time you took flight."

"But what about you?"

"Oh, child, it's time I took flight, too, but I'm not going with y'all."

Janie frowned. "Where you going?"

Aunty Mil stopped eating and aimed her sightless eyes in Janie's direction. "I'm going to heaven, baby."

"When?"

"When my Maker comes get me, that's when."

Janie sat very still. She felt afraid. "But when's that, Aunty?"

Aunty Mil didn't speak at first. All that could be heard was her spoon scraping the bowl. Finally she spoke. "Oh, that was good. Now come take my bowl, child. Let Aunty tell you about it." Janie scurried over to relieve the old woman of her dish and spoon.

"Now see here." Aunty Mil found Janie's head and rubbed on it with her bony fingers. Janie sank to her knees beside the chair and felt instantly comforted.

"Janie-bird, my time here is near about done. I know it. I feel it. I dream about it 'most every night. I don't know when my time to leave will be, but it will be soon enough. And then I got to go. Aunty Mil gonna fly right on outta this cabin, right up over this plantation, and right on up to heaven. You understand?"

Janie knew a little something about heaven. Her mother had introduced her to Jesus before Janie was taken to Shannon Oaks, and Janie believed that Jesus lived in her own heart. She hadn't given a lot of thought to heaven, though. She had heard songs about heaven sung all her life, first by Momma in their cabin, then secretly in the pine groves when she came to Rubyhill. During the frightening days of slavery, it had been illegal and dangerous for slaves to gather for any reason without the watchful eye of white men. Some slaves were even killed for it.

But most slaves believed in God, and many of them met together secretly for church. They gathered in groves of trees that would deaden the sound of their preaching and singing. That's where Janie mostly heard about heaven. She recalled hearing words much like Aunty Mil's, and there were plenty of songs about it. But Janie did not always know what those words meant exactly, even when she sang them herself.

The old woman went on. "Aunty Mil's been walking this creation a long, long time. This body's near about ready to give out. And when it's time, I'm leaving this old body behind. It will happen. You know this, Janie-bird. Heaven's my true home. I want to go home to my Maker and my family gone on before me. I don't want to leave you here, baby girl, but I got to go."

Aunty Mil turned to the fire. "And I been thinking on this for a long time, that you got to get north. You shouldn't stay here in Georgia no-how. Now you got your chance to fly on outta here with the others. I got to go where I'm going, baby girl, and I'll meet you on the other side. For now, though, you got to get north."

This was a lot for Janie to take in, and she felt afraid again. Ever since Janie was taken from Momma, Aunty Mil had been her family. "No, Aunty, I won't leave you."

Aunty Mil continued stroking Janie's head as if she were a cat. "Mm-mm-mm," she said. "That's all right, child." Janie could hear a smile in her voice. She leaned her face against Aunty Mil's apron. "Don't you worry," Aunty cooed.

The cabin became quiet with only the sounds of Aunty's rocking chair, the crackling fire, and the raspy breathing of the old woman.

"Sing me that song, child."

"Which one, Aunty?"

"The one about going to Canaan-land."

Janie began to sing the much-loved spiritual. She was known around the quarters for having a high, sweet voice, clear as a bird, according to Aunty Mil. Janie closed her eyes and sang her young heart out. When she was done, she saw Aunty Mil had dozed off. Janie watched the old woman's thin body rise and fall with the sounds of her breath.

Singing always helped Janie feel better. Now she felt hungry again. Aunty Mil was in the middle of her nap, resting nicely, so Janie took her own bowl of mush outside to eat it.

As she ate, Janie thought over what Aunty Mil had said about going to heaven. She'd heard other old ones talk like that but hadn't ever paid much attention to their words until now. When was Aunty Mil going away? Why did she have to leave at all?

Janie scraped her bowl with her spoon and tucked the dish inside the cabin door to clean later. She headed up the path toward the Big House. She needed to talk to Aleta.

When she reached the front yard, Janie heard her name called. She spun around to find Aleta hurrying toward her.

Aleta was excited. "Come on up here about dusk. Some of us are meeting by the kitchen to make plans for going north." Aleta's eyes looked very bright.

But Janie could not respond. She turned and ran back down the path. When Aleta called after her, Janie just ran faster, hurrying back to the warm security of the cabin and Aunty Mil.

Once inside, Janie saw that the fire needed tending. She rummaged for some small pieces of wood, keeping as quiet as possible for the sake of the sleeping Aunty Mil.

Janie stoked the fire and then grabbed a pail to fetch water at the pump. Only then did she realize there was no sound coming from the rocking chair.

Janie slowly walked to Aunty Mil and reached for the old woman's hand. It was cold.

"Aunty Mil?"

There was no answer.

Shannon Oaks Plantation, Georgia

Anna swept her cabin's dirt floor, steering the stray pieces of straw and chunks of mud to the small fireplace. She hummed softly to herself, a tune she'd learned from her own mother. Anna never knew the words to the song, but the melody always sounded hopeful to her.

And Anna lived daily with the hope of tomorrow. It was the best she could do. Hope was all she had left.

But at least the bondage was over, praise the Lord. She would never again be anyone's slave. And if there were any earthly way, George would find her again, he would.

After all, who would have believed Master would have had to let them all go free here at Shannon Oaks? Never would anyone have believed that could happen. And if that could happen all over the land, George could come back to her. And then they could go find their daughter.

She thought of George, whom she'd not seen now for seven long years. Big strong George with skin the color of strong coffee with just a touch of milk stirred in. That's what she always told him. His dark eyes would light up every time she said that.

Anna sighed. How she missed George. And how she missed their singing, brown-eyed girl whom she'd not seen in six years. Anna prayed one prayer daily: "Dear Lord, I thank You for life for one more day. I ask for George and my baby to come back to me. In Jesus' name I pray this."

She went back to sweeping and humming. One day closer to seeing her loved ones again. That's what she had to believe.

CHAPTER 5

The Burial

Janie sat on the small woodpile outside the cabin she shared with Aunty Mil and pulled her knees up to her chin. She wrapped her arms around her thin legs and put her head on her knees.

Inside the cabin, two women prepared the old woman for her burial. They worked quietly. Everyone had loved Aunty Mil.

Aleta trotted down the path from the Big House. "Oh, Janie," she said, "I just heard." She grabbed Janie's hand.

Janie squeezed Aleta's hand for a minute then pulled her own hand back. Again she wrapped her arms around her legs.

Aleta sank down next to Janie on the woodpile. "You all right?" she asked in a gentle tone.

Janie shook her head. She could not speak.

That was a familiar feeling, the stark fear in her heart coupled with the inability to speak. She remembered when she'd first come to Rubyhill six years ago, how frightened and silent she had been.

Only five years old and ripped away from her home for the first time in her young life, Janie had been terrified by the time she entered the back drive at Rubyhill. All her life, she'd been safe and sound with Momma, or so she'd thought. But suddenly she had been yanked away by strange white people, thrown into a wagon full of other child slaves, taken away to a place she'd never seen, and thrust into the hands of more people she did not know.

When the black people at Rubyhill asked Janie her name that day, she stared back at them, too frightened to speak. They were very kind to the little girl. They understood all too well the shock of being pulled away from family, never to return. But when they asked her questions, Janie simply could not speak. She even opened her mouth to try. It was as if no sound would come out of her.

That's when Old Joe picked her up and carried her to Aunty Mil's cabin. The old blind woman had felt the top of Janie's head with her soft dry hand. Then she'd stroked Janie's braids gently, cooing at her the whole time. Janie remembered it well.

"You just a little bit of a thing," Aunty Mil had said to her, chuckling softly. "You just a little dickens, ain't you? And they all say you can't talk. Well, old Aunty Mill thinks you just not ready. I can't see you or nothin' else, baby girl, so some time, you got to talk to me so's we can know each other. Meantime, though, you stay here in Aunty Mil's cabin, and you don't ever got to move again. Hear me?"

Little Janie had nodded. Only then did it dawn on her that the old woman couldn't see her nod. But Aunty Mil had felt Janie's head move under her hand, and she'd laughed out loud. "We gonna do just fine, you and me. You'll talk to Aunty when you's good and ready."

It had been months before little Janie had spoken. She had silently performed any chore asked of her. She worked hard for the cook at the Big House, fetching things from the root cellar, washing fruits and vegetables at the pump, climbing into low cupboards or up onto high shelves to get pots and pans the heavyset cook couldn't reach. And every night back at the cabin, Aunty Mil had stroked Janie's hair and prayed out loud as the child fell asleep.

One morning as Janie was waking up, Aunty Mil tripped on the broom in the cabin. The old woman fell and landed in the fireplace, and her skirt caught fire. Little Janie quickly beat the fire out with a small skillet, but Aunty Mil's legs were burned. "Quick, baby, go get someone!" the old woman told her.

Frightened, Janie had run outside in the quarters and not known where to go or what to do. It was still dark out. So she used her voice for the first time at Rubyhill. It was squeaky, but it worked. Little Janie stood in the middle of the center path and called out in her high voice: "Help! Help! Aunty's hurt!"

The other slaves poured out of their cabins and ran to her. Janie pointed inside the cabin, and Aunty Mil was quickly helped. The women in the quarters brought healing herbs and cooling salves to treat the burns. Before long, Aunty Mil's burns got better and went away, leaving only some raised scars on her leg.

But what truly made the old woman happy was that Janie had spoken out loud to help her. Janie never stopped talking after that. She even began to sing.

Of course, once Aunty Mil heard Janie sing, Janie had to sing all the time. Her sweet, high melodies filled the cabin, and on warm nights, the entire quarter was given the gift of her songs, traveling on the heavy air.

Aunty Mil often prayed out loud her thanks to God for having been burned because that's when Janie's sweet voice was "loosed." That's how Aunty Mil put it. And that's when she started calling the child Janie-bird.

Of course, it also meant the two could talk to each other at last. And talk they did! "You remember, child," Aunty Mil often said, "the Lord can make a way out of no way. Aunty Mil got hurt, but you and your birdsong sprung up out of it all. The Lord made it good."

Now Janie sat in silence with Aleta and let the memories stir around inside her heart and mind. What good could come of this? She couldn't believe Aunty Mil lay dead inside the cabin. It hurt so much.

Finally Aleta spoke. "Don't get quiet again, little sis. Don't stop talking and singing. Aunty wouldn't want that."

Janie stared at the ground and said nothing.

The two women came out of the cabin. One squatted down before Janie. "Baby, we gonna bury Aunty Mil pretty soon. We got her all nice and ready. You want to come in and sit a spell with her?"

Janie didn't move. Aleta gently pried one of Janie's hands away from clutching the other hand and pulled her up. "Come on, little sis. Let's say good-bye."

Aleta led Janie into the cabin where Aunty Mil lay stretched out on her pallet. Janie still stared down at the dirt floor. Aleta knelt next to the old woman and pulled Janie down next to her.

Janie felt the fire at her back. She was afraid to look at Aunty Mil.

"Come on, Janie," Aleta coaxed. "We got to say good-bye to Aunty Mil."

Janie finally raised her eyes to look at the old woman. Aunty Mil was lying perfectly straight and still, her hands folded on her chest. Janie stared, wondering what was so different. Then she realized that she had never seen Aunty's body straight or still. The old woman had had so many aches and pains that she could not even lie down. Aunty slept in the rocker. And even in her sleep, she moaned and moved about. Now she clearly was without pain.

Janie crept closer to Aunty Mil. The women had taken the kerchief off her head, and Janie saw Aunty Mil's long white braids spread out. She looked so young! It even looked like she was slightly smiling. Janie was amazed. Truly the real Aunty Mil had left her body and gone away, just like she said she would.

Aleta leaned closer to Janie. "You all right?"

Janie nodded. She still could not speak. She didn't know how she was going to get along without Aunty Mil, but she did know in her heart that the old woman was in a better place. She was glad about that. She reached out and touched the soft skin on Aunty Mil's cheek. Then she sat back and waited.

Soon the women came back in and wound long, white sheets around Aunty Mil. Then two men came in and picked up the ends of the sheets. They carried Aunty Mil's body outside and placed her on a cart drawn by a mule. The entire community of former slaves gathered behind the wagon. They followed the slow-moving mule and cart to the graveyard, where two men with shovels waited by a freshly dug grave. Aleta began to sing, and the others joined in.

Janie felt numb as she followed close behind the wagon. At the grave, she stood and held onto the white sheets at Aunty Mil's feet while Old Joe said a few words. She could feel the pewter cross under her dress, resting against her skin. It was a comfort to feel it.

Lost in her own thoughts, Janie didn't pay much attention to Old Joe until he addressed her directly. "Little Janie, you know Aunty Mil loved to hear you sing. You sing for her, would you now?"

Janie's heart felt like it would break. But Old Joe was right. And she knew Aunty would not want her to hide in silence ever again. So Janie began to sing, her high notes climbing and soaring over the pine trees. She saw Old Joe wipe his eyes. Then she closed her own eyes as Aunty Mil's body was lowered into the ground.

The men shoveled dirt into the grave. This was hard for Janie to watch. Again she felt the pewter cross press against her, and again, it was a comfort. She touched the outline of the cross through her dress.

When the grave was filled, a mound of dirt remained on top. Each of Rubyhill's former slaves found a rock nearby and placed it on the mound. Janie found a speckled rock, and she placed her rock on the pile, too.

When it was all over, the others moved silently back to work. Old Joe stayed behind and looked at Aunty Mil's grave for a long time. Then he patted Janie's head and turned down the path toward the quarters. Aleta stayed with Janie.

Janie finally spoke. "What am I gonna do now?"

"You know what you gonna do, little sis. You goin' north with us."

Janie looked at Aleta. "And leave her here in the ground?"

"Oh, Janie," said Aleta, "Aunty knew she was goin' on. And she knew we's goin' north. Don't you think maybe she and God worked it out so you don't have to stay and worry over her no more?"

Janie considered this. In spite of her sadness, she had to smile. "You might be right about that," she said to Aleta. "She wanted me to go north. And she was mighty happy about goin' to heaven. Said it was her time."

The two girls gazed at the mound of dirt awhile longer. Then Janie picked a nearby branch and laid it on the mound of dirt and rocks. "Good-bye, Aunty Mil. You sure been good to me. I will see you in heaven some day."

The two girls turned and walked hand-in-hand back to the quarters.

"Stay with me tonight, Janie," said Aleta. "Don't go back to the cabin by yourself."

Janie considered this. "I'll stay with you, Aleta—but first I got to go back to the cabin and get something."

"Want me to come along?"

"If you like. I thank you."

The girls trudged silently down the path to Aunty Mil's cabin.

Inside the cabin, Aleta busied herself rolling Janie's blanket and setting aside pans to take. Janie looked around. She knew she would not be back.

She spied the broken rocker. A wave of emotion swept over the young girl, knowing Aunty Mil truly was gone and would never rock in that chair again.

Janie walked over to the hearth and found the paring knife. Then she sliced a large square of fabric from the rocking chair. She cut it from the back ruffle so that more stuffing wouldn't come out. Surely someone else would want to use the chair. She folded the square of fabric and stuffed it into her skirt pocket.

"Lookie here," said Aleta. "You might want this."

Janie turned to see Aleta standing next to the hearth, holding out Aunty Mil's pale yellow head scarf. Janie took the scarf from Aleta, held it to her face, and breathed in the smell of Aunty Mil's hair.

A memory came to Janie, distinct and sweet. Every week, she and Aunty Mil would unbraid and rebraid one another's hair. Aunty Mil had taught her how to braid when Janie first arrived at Rubyhill. The old woman had placed her own cool, bony fingers over Janie's tiny ones and taught her first with string. It was awhile before she let the little girl braid real hair.

But Aunty Mil braided Janie's hair from the beginning, always telling her Bible stories, offering her a look at life that would train the child well. "Jesus walked this earth, child, so that He would know what it's like bein' a man," Aunty Mil instructed the girl. "He came down here to save us and free us. Then He went back to heaven to be with His Father. From up there, Jesus helps you. All you got to do is ask. You remember that."

Janie did remember it. Now she took the folded kerchief and placed it in her pocket next to the fabric square. Then Aleta and Janie stepped out of the cabin forever.

CHAPTER 6

A Harvest Moon

Janie woke up with a start. *Where am I?*

The full harvest moon shone so brightly that for a moment Janie thought it was dawn. But it was not. It only felt that way because she was sleeping outside in the light of that huge moon filtering through tree branches overhead.

Quickly Janie remembered why she was sleeping outside. She was part of the small party of Rubyhill's young former slaves who had left the plantation and were now moving north. They had just walked all day, resting only occasionally until they stopped at the edge of this cedar forest. There they'd eaten supper and fallen asleep as darkness came on. It was their first night away from home.

The fire was reduced to only coals. Janie sat up and listened to the sounds of the woods next to them. It was nerve-racking, hearing all those outdoor sounds so close by—owls hooting, small creatures scurrying, leaves rustling, and who knew what else—and nothing to keep any of it at bay. Janie hoped it was true what they said, that snakes don't crawl at night. She did wonder, though.

Janie wrapped her blanket tightly around herself and looked about. Sleeping around the fire wrapped in their own blankets were four others—Aleta, Lucy, Nathan, and Blue. When it came down to actually leaving, these five were the only ones who decided to go north.

Janie thought about why they were the only ones going. Maybe it was because none of them would have to leave family behind. Blue had been sold to Rubyhill from some place in Virginia when he was very young. Aleta was born at Rubyhill, but all her kin were gone. Nathan and Lucy only had each other. They'd come to Rubyhill the same time as Janie, and they remembered little about their original family.

Janie's mind wandered to the events of the last week. So much had happened: Miz Laura's departure, Old Joe finding the box of Yankee cash, then the death of dear Aunty Mil. The five young former slaves had waited only until the second day after the burial before venturing out.

Janie had dragged her feet at the thought of leaving so soon after losing Aunty Mil. So much was changing so fast. But the elders insisted that it was important to leave while the full moon offered so much light. Blue also reminded Janie that soon autumn would turn to winter. "We need to get as far north as we can before snow falls," Blue insisted. "Old Joe's told me how to go, and we got to go right away."

So Janie went along with it. They began making plans the day after Aunty Mil's death. All the other former slaves at Rubyhill prepared food for their young people for the journey—easy things to carry like hard-boiled eggs, pecans, boiled peanuts, and dried apricots. They distributed squares of cornbread and gingerbread to be stuffed into pockets for nibbling along the way. They even slaughtered and fried up one of Rubyhill's few chickens for their young people to take. Janie's mouth still drooled at the memory of how tasty that cold fried chicken had been at suppertime.

The five young ones also packed and carried a skillet, a boiling pot, a chopping knife, and some burlap bags of rice and cornmeal. Each one brought his or her own cup, bowl, and spoon. Blue wore a pouch around his waist and under his clothes in which he carried most of the Yankee cash. The rest of the cash was divided up among the other four and tucked deep into their pockets in case they somehow became separated along the way.

Early that morning, Aleta had distributed footwear and jackets taken from the Big House, items to be worn later when it turned cold. Each of the five young people rolled these garments up in his or her own blanket, which was about all any of them owned besides the clothes on their backs. They even slept in those clothes.

Janie brought along three more personal things. She wore the pewter cross under her dress, and she kept both the square of fabric from Aunty Mil's rocking chair and Aunty's pale yellow kerchief folded in her pocket.

Janie thought about how they left the plantation all in a line: Blue in the lead, Aleta at the end. All of Rubyhill's former slaves walked to the outskirts of the plantation with them to see them off. Some of the elders had begun to weep as Old Joe said a prayer over the five young people and sent them on their way.

As the five travelers began walking away, Cookie started to sing one of Janie's favorite songs, and the other former slaves joined in:

"If I could I surely would
Stand on the rock where Moses stood.
Pharaoh's army got drown–ded,
Oh, Mary, don't you weep. . . ."

For a long while, Janie, Blue, Aleta, Lucy, and Nathan could hear the singing voices of those who had been the only family they had.

Now, by the light of the dying coals and the vibrant moon, Janie reached into her pocket and pulled out the yellow kerchief. She held it to her face and breathed in that familiar smell of Aunty Mil's hair. It was a living smell, sharp and sweet.

Janie placed the kerchief back in her pocket. She wrapped her blanket tighter around herself and rocked. She cried without making a sound.

Shannon Oaks Plantation, Georgia

Anna tended the supper fire in her cabin in silence. A full harvest moon had slowly made its way up and over Shannon Oaks.

It had been a long day of fieldwork. After supper, Anna intended to go right to sleep and rest up for another long day. Maybe she'd dream of her little girl again.

Georgeanna. Born Christmas Day and named after her parents. Her pretty little baby with the pretty name.

Back then, when Master's young wife had heard the new baby's name, she'd said, "That's too fine a name for a black baby. You call her Janie."

So Anna had no choice but to call her baby Janie. At least the woman liked Anna, or she, too, would have been sold south, probably soon after George was sold.

Word back then was that the soil at Shannon Oaks had become tired. That's how the men put it, anyway. They meant that the soil wasn't working as well as it used to, so the plantation wasn't producing the amount of quality cotton and tobacco it once had.

But Master was used to high living. And high living did not come cheap. To continue his standard of living, Master started dealing in and selling livestock, concentrating on horses. Then he concentrated on selling human beings. Even five-year-old Janie.

But not Anna. Master's wife absolutely would not allow it. And Master hated it when his young wife was unhappy. Nevertheless, he continued selling the other slaves, so that by wartime, not many were left at Shannon Oaks.

Anna's thoughts were interrupted by the loud bray of a mule outside. She didn't recognize this mule's bray, and it sounded like it was close by.

She stood and peeked out her cabin door. There in the bright moonlight stood a very thin man holding the reins of a mule in one hand and a bunch of sunflowers in the other. He stepped toward the cabin door.

Now Anna could see the man better. And—oh, could it be? Did he have skin the color of strong coffee with just a touch of milk stirred in?

The thin man's face broke out into a wide smile. "Anna?"

Anna's knees gave way, and she sank gently to the ground. It was George. Alive. He had come back to her, just as he promised he would.

George ran and dropped to the ground beside his wife, cradling her in his arms. Seven long years were over in one moment as both of them sobbed openly with joy.

CHAPTER 7

The Rubyhill Five

On the third day of the journey north, clouds filled up the sky. Soon enough, a cold rain poured on the little band from Rubyhill. *Seems like every step we take north, things get colder,* Janie thought. *Even rain.*

The plan was to reach Chicago before winter set in. That was a distance that should take them about forty days on foot, according to Old Joe. They would move north by northwest through Georgia, then into Tennessee, Kentucky, and Indiana. Old Joe pointed out that Chicago "sits right on top of Indiana." Janie didn't quite understand what that meant, and Blue explained that it meant it was at the northern point of Indiana.

Old Joe sat them down for a talk the day before they left. He warned them that there could be snow once they hit Indiana. "You might have to sit out a snowstorm but not too much, leastways not till after the first of the year. Remember, winter moves south faster than you can walk north. You got to keep moving and get to Chicago long before Christmas."

He warned them that once they got into Chicago, the cold wind would be brutal. "You young'uns ain't got the blood for that now, but you will by the next winter. The blood thickens up after you been in the cold awhile. First winter, though, y'all gonna feel the chill right down to your bones 'cause y'all from Georgia. But you remember Old Joe said it's gonna get better."

That had not sounded at all appealing to Janie. Already on this trip, she was feeling colder at night than she remembered ever being before.

The Rubyhill Five had skirted Atlanta and now found themselves close to Tennessee on this rainy third day of travel. They filed silently through an open pasture bordered by wooded hills and boulders. As they neared the tree line, Aleta spoke up. "We got to put off walking for now, Blue," she said. "Won't do no good to take sick in this wet cold."

Blue nodded and stopped in his tracks. Janie marveled at what a good team those two made. One made a suggestion; the other either agreed or reasoned out something else. Janie, Nathan, and Lucy rarely needed to express their opinions under the leadership of this almost adult teamwork. They just let themselves be led by Aleta and Blue.

Aleta spied a huge boulder with an overhang of rock. The grass under it was long and looked fairly dry. "Let's try that over there."

The five moved as one to duck under the rocky overhang. They slid down onto the grass together. "Move in closer," said Aleta. They huddled against one another until the rain could reach only their bare toes.

"Sure wish I'da thought to bring some kinda oilcloth for this rain," groused Blue. "All I thought about was snow."

"All I thought about was food," said Aleta. They both chuckled at that, and Nathan and Lucy giggled right along. Janie felt grateful that the group tended to stay in such high spirits even in the face of difficulties.

The route Old Joe had mapped out for them was working out so far. They were covering probably close to twenty miles each day, just as Joe thought they might. Over and over he warned them they should keep moving while both good weather and food lasted. The food was holding out so far, but they would have to start foraging for more in a couple of days.

The quiet chatter stopped eventually, and the youths leaned against each other for about half an hour. Janie felt herself getting sleepy in the gentle sounds of the rain. Her head dropped on Aleta's shoulder.

"Listen," she heard Nathan whisper.

It was the sound of thrashing grass. Someone or something was out there in the rain. Quite a lot of someone or something, it sounded like.

Aleta turned to Blue. "Deer?" she whispered anxiously.

Blue shook his head. "Men," he whispered back.

The five ex-slaves knew that avoiding contact with white people on this trip would be good. Yes, blacks were free now. But not all white folks were happy about that.

Janie had often heard the elders back at Rubyhill talk about the state of affairs these days. Rubyhill wasn't the only place where people had to scrape to get food to eat, they reported. Nobody fared all that well anywhere in the South, and some white people blamed black people for the hardships. Those white people sometimes took the law into their own hands to hurt black people. The elders had said that the law of the land had never protected blacks before, and there was still no reason to expect it to. "Maybe some day, Lord willing," Janie had heard Old Joe say. "But that day ain't here yet."

So the band of five moved fairly quietly most of the time, and they stayed away from main roads and houses. Besides, they didn't want to get accused of trespassing on anyone's land.

The thrashing came closer. Then voices. Deep male voices. Janie felt afraid. She closed her eyes and touched the outline of the pewter cross beneath her dress. *Please protect us, Jesus. . . .*

"You head on home, buddy, and start on those chores," she heard a man say. "We'll be along shortly."

A younger voice replied, "Yes, sir."

The thrashing moved away. Janie was so relieved she thought she'd faint. Instead, she opened her eyes and found herself looking straight up into the face of a tall white boy, maybe fifteen or sixteen. She could feel everyone else look up, too. The boy carried a rifle.

Seeing them gave him a start, and he stared back, mouth open. For a long while, nobody spoke. They could hear the voices of the other men fade into the distance, but nobody moved or said a word.

Janie took in the young man's appearance. Even in her fear, she noticed that his clothes were wool. He wore boots and a red hat, and hanging off his belt was a very fat rabbit he'd apparently shot. The boy's eyes were bright blue.

It was as if everyone, black and white, were struck mute. When they could no longer hear the men in the distance, the white boy finally spoke. "Y'all hungry?"

Nobody moved except Nathan. He nodded.

The white boy untied the rabbit and threw it to Nathan, who reached up and caught it in the air. "Y'all have to skin it yerself," the white boy said. Then he grinned, turned, and jogged off in the rain.

Nathan stood up. He triumphantly held the rabbit up high. Rainwater dripped off it.

"Well, I'll be," said Blue. "I'll be."

"Nice white boy, sure enough, but we still trespassin'," Aleta reminded him nervously. "We got to move on soon as this rain lets up."

So they did. Several miles later, the rain stopped completely. Blue spied a tobacco barn that appeared abandoned. "We'll sleep here tonight," he said.

"We best build a supper fire elsewhere," said Aleta.

Blue nodded and took off walking. "Start skinnin' that rabbit!" he called over his shoulder. "And find us some dry kindling, too! I'll be back."

Aleta worked on the rabbit, and the others silently foraged for dry firewood. By the time Blue came back, they were ready to cook. Then Blue led them a quarter mile away to the place he'd scouted out for the supper fire.

Aleta made an excellent rice stew with the rabbit. It was a welcome and rare hot meal for the weary travelers. By the time they'd trudged back to the tobacco barn, Janie thought she'd fall asleep on her feet.

Stomachs full of hot food, all five young people fell fast asleep in their blankets.

Shannon Oaks Plantation, Georgia

Anna stirred honey into a pot of oats that hung in the fireplace. She turned to her husband. "I still got to fatten you up, mister."

George sat on the cabin floor and grinned. His eyes sparkled in the firelight. "No complaints, woman."

"That's good," Anna replied. She bent over the fire and began dropping mounds of dough into a flat skillet on top of the coals.

George chuckled. "I been dreamin' about them biscuits for seven years now."

Anna flashed a smile at her once-strong husband. His complexion looked better after four days of rest and food, but he was still so thin. He'd arrived at Shannon Oaks weak and not able to keep any food down for the first couple of days. Once he was able to digest Anna's baked custard, he'd been improving ever since. Good thing he was still young. He would recover his strength.

Anna's gratitude at having George back could hardly be described. Her heartfelt prayers of thanksgiving were constant. She wondered what had happened in George's life all these years, but there was no hurry to share difficult stories.

Of course, they had right away talked about little Janie. George had understandably been stunned to hear his daughter was gone. Now he brought it up again. "I still can't get over it, Anna. What these white folks thinkin', sellin' off a little girl like Janie?"

Anna turned back to the fire and hung her head. The day her child had been taken from her was the most powerless day of Anna's life.

George reached over and grabbed his wife's hand. "Listen here. You couldn't do nothin' about it," he said. "You stayed strong like I asked." George stroked Anna's work-worn fingers. "Now I'll be your strength," he said. "We'll find our girl."

Anna sighed. "No telling where she is now."

George considered this. "You say they took her to Rubyhill. She might still be there. If not, someone there will know something. Let's you and me rest up a couple more days, and we'll head out for Rubyhill."

Anna looked into George's eyes. "You sure you up to it?"

George nodded. "We got to find our girl."

"Yes, Lord help us," said Anna.

Three days later, George and Anna left Shannon Oaks. A kind network of former slaves living in a dozen plantations along the way directed them in their journey to Rubyhill. It was two counties away in unfamiliar territory.

But along the way, each plantation's slave quarters opened up to the couple and showed them the best hospitality. At every turn, a community fed them and gave them a place to stay for the night.

By the time George and Anna reached Rubyhill three days later, they were anxious with anticipation and dread. Was little Janie here?

They approached the main grounds of Rubyhill slowly, steering toward the slave quarters. It was always best for black people to avoid white people when approaching a strange plantation.

"Don't seem to be no whites 'round here," remarked George.

Anna nodded. "Let's go to the kitchen."

Good smells wafted from the detached kitchen. As they drew closer, a heavyset woman stepped out and looked them over.

"How you folks?" she said. She gave the couple a friendly, gap-toothed smile.

Anna smiled back. George doffed his hat to the cook. "My name's George, and this here's my wife, Anna."

The women nodded to each other.

George continued. "We's looking for our little girl. She got sold from under us over at Shannon Oaks some six years ago. We heard she was brought over here."

"What's her name?" asked the cook.

"Her name's Janie," said Anna. "She's goin' on twelve years come Christmas—"

"Janie?" The cook looked stunned. "Oh, honey, Janie just left here, not even a week ago."

Anna grabbed George's arm. "What you mean?" she asked the cook.

"Five of our young'uns took off north to get themselves work. You just missed your girl, honey."

Anna's knees buckled. She felt George grab her up in his arms to keep her on her feet. She heard him say to the cook, "Ma'am, do you know where they's headed?"

"Chicago's what was said," the cook responded.

Anna no longer heard the conversation. She simply sank to the ground.

So close. So close, and so far.

CHAPTER 8

Maydean

Janie was weary. Bone weary. She concentrated on putting one foot in front of the other. Surely they would stop and rest soon.

Around thirty days had passed, and the Rubyhill Five had been on the road a long time—too long for Janie. It was late October, and she didn't know how much longer she could take it. But they still had to get through the whole state of Indiana.

The five young people had crossed the state line from Kentucky to Indiana just that morning. Every day they were closer to Chicago than they were the day before, but it seemed like every day they moved a little slower.

Janie was getting worried. Days were so cold and nights even colder. They were running into brief snow squalls here and there. They had begun wearing the heavy coats they'd found in the Big House. They were even wearing shoes and socks, and although the shoes felt uncomfortable to feet unused to footwear, everybody's feet stayed dry and warm.

Today the Rubyhill Five experienced autumn in Indiana as they'd never experienced it in Georgia. Everywhere the maple trees were vibrant with color. Janie had never seen anything like it—leaves that were bright yellow and red and some kind of color in between. She'd gathered a few at first but had since let them flutter back to the ground. There were so many.

But the thrill of all that beauty soon wore off. Janie was too cold and tired to care about nature's beauty. She was more concerned about how difficult nature was making it for them to get to their destination.

One of the biggest issues was food. Once again, Janie felt that constant, gnawing hunger. All the carrying food was gone, and foraging for food every day took time and energy. They worked hard for every bite they ate.

Fortunately, apples were in season and plentiful along the way, but how they all longed for—and needed—a good hot meal. *Maybe some chicken stew and biscuits,* Janie thought as she trudged along. *With boiled potatoes and carrots. Maybe some fried apple pie. Maybe. . .*

Janie stopped herself. This would do nothing but make her hungrier. She continued concentrating on taking each step.

There was one more worrisome thing, the most worrisome thing of all. Blue was coughing. It had started a couple days ago, and it seemed like every hour the cough sounded deeper and rougher.

Aleta fussed over him about it that morning. "Blue, that cough sounds evil. Let's take a day off and let you get some strength."

Blue showed a rare display of anger. "What we supposed to do, then?" he snapped. "All of us lay down 'til I get better? We ain't got that kinda time, and we ain't got nowhere to lay down. We got to keep going."

Aleta protested but soon said nothing more. Janie felt a little sick to her stomach to hear these two argue. She and Nathan and Lucy exchanged glances from time to time but remained quiet all morning.

The morning stretched on until Aleta insisted they stop at a maple grove and look for food. Blue said nothing. Instead, he stepped off the path and sank down onto the thick roots of a large tree. Janie saw that he was shivering.

As troubling as it was to see Blue this way, the three younger ones immediately circled out from the grove looking around for water and for something to eat. They left Blue with Aleta, who busied herself unpacking cookware and apples.

Nathan found some field corn, the kind livestock ate, but it would be better than nothing. They stuffed ears of it in their pockets. Then Lucy found mushrooms. After they determined the mushrooms were safe—they knew which ones were poison-ous—the three picked lots of them. They also found hickory nuts and a creek from which they drew water with their boiling pots.

After an hour, they knew this would have to do. It wasn't a lot, but they could eat and still keep walking. They headed back to the maple grove. As they neared, Janie heard Lucy gasp. Janie looked up. Blue was stretched out on the ground. Aleta had wrapped him in his blanket, and he was shivering violently.

The three approached slowly. Aleta looked up and saw them. "Come help me keep this blanket on Blue. He's shakin' it right back off."

They all managed to get the blanket wrapped more tightly around Blue, who was indeed shaking terribly. Then Aleta had them all huddle around Blue to see if he could get warm enough to stop shivering. The five were used to huddling together by this point on the journey. But in this huddle, Janie could actually feel the feverish heat emanate from Blue.

Janie touched the outline of the pewter cross under her clothes as she did so often these days and began to pray silently. *Lord, help*

Blue. Help us all, Lord. We in trouble.

They stayed together under the tree all afternoon. Nobody talked, and nobody ate. Blue began to moan in his fever. Aleta looked terribly frightened, though she tried not to appear so. Nobody asked the question they all had on their minds: *What now?*

Dark came earlier every day this time of year, and it was fast approaching. Clearly there would be no more travel today. Still, nobody moved from huddling around Blue.

Finally Aleta spoke. "Each of you, one at a time, go fetch your blankets and come on back. We gonna stay close together tonight. We gonna get some water down this boy, and then y'all need to drink and eat what you found, right here in the huddle."

So that's what they did. Blue's fever actually kept them all warm throughout the night, but it was not a comfort by any means. Blue eventually became delirious, talking nonsense and even laughing in his feverish state. Nobody slept well under the circumstances.

Janie woke up with the cold morning sunlight touching her face. She looked around. The others still dozed, huddled up against Blue, who had finally fallen asleep. His breathing was loud and heavy.

Janie gently extricated herself from the sleeping tangle of the Rubyhill Five. She didn't want to wake anyone. But she was hungry. As she munched on mushrooms and hickory nuts from yesterday's food search, she decided to build a fire for boiling apples.

Moving quietly, Janie left the maple grove to search for kindling. At the edge of the noisy creek they'd found yesterday, she sensed she was not alone. She turned in a slow circle, her gaze darting about until she spied what she'd sensed was there.

Only a few yards away stood a white girl wearing a heavy jacket, men's pants, and big boots. She had the reddest hair Janie had ever seen. It was long and curly, and Janie saw that it was very matted. Janie had not heard this girl approach.

The two looked at each other for a moment. Then the redheaded girl spoke. "You're not from 'round here. Where you from?"

Janie was very startled by this. "Georgia," she replied.

"Where's that?" said the white girl.

Not sure how to answer, Janie paused. "Down south," she finally said.

"Who are you?"

On this journey, the Rubyhill Five had determined to keep information to a minimum when dealing with local whites and to keep on moving. They had not yet had anything frightening happen to them at the hands of locals, but it could happen. Janie told the redheaded girl her name and nothing else.

The girl spoke again. "You all alone?"

Janie paused, then shook her head.

The girl considered this. "My name's Maydean. I live down the holler with my granddaddy. He's drunk all the time and mean as a snake." She stopped talking, as if she'd said too much. "You movin' on through?"

Janie nodded. "Going north."

"Where 'bouts?"

"Chicago."

"I heard of it," the girl said. Janie saw that she was probably around her own age. The girl had the same shockingly blue eyes as that boy who had given them the rabbit. Janie noted wearily that it seemed like that had happened a long time ago.

The girl stepped forward. "What you doin' here?"

"Looking for firewood."

"I'll help you." And with that, the white girl tromped about in her pants and boots, briskly picking up small pieces of wood and stuffing them into her jacket pocket. Janie drew a little closer and noticed that the girl's clothes were filthy. She could see that the girl was very thin and that the dirty clothes hung loosely on her.

After about ten minutes, the two had enough wood to build a fire and sustain it for boiling a pot of apples. Janie wondered what she should do now. Did she dare take this white girl back to her sleeping friends, especially when one of them was clearly sick?

Then it occurred to Janie that maybe this Maydean was the answer to the praying she'd been doing all night. The redhead seemed an unlikely answer to prayer, so Janie prayed one more thing silently: *Lord?*

Janie had the strongest impression that she should invite Maydean to eat with her and the others. Yet that was a very foolish thing to consider. Whites and blacks absolutely never, ever ate together. Janie could offer, but the girl would most likely refuse.

Nevertheless, Janie decided to invite her to share their food. "Maydean, are you hungry?"

Maydean's face was unreadable. Then she nodded. It suddenly occurred to Janie that if Maydean lived with a drunken granddaddy, she might be hungry a lot of the time.

"Come on, then," said Janie, and she led the redhead to the maple grove.

Rubyhill Plantation, Georgia

George and Anna never returned to Shannon Oaks. Instead, the hospitable Rubyhill residents took care of them for the next week and helped them plan their own trip to Chicago.

"You might as well stay here and get ready for your journey north," Old Joe had reasoned with George and Anna. "You cain't catch up with them others no-how. They all young and got a head start over you two. They say a black man live high as a white man up there in Chicago these days. I'll tell you everything I know 'bout getting up there, everything I told them children. You'll find your girl up there. But it's a mighty long way, and fella,"—Old Joe directed this to George—"I don't know's you should start it right away no-how."

Cook led George and Anna to Aunty Mil's now-empty cabin. The women had swept out the fireplace and the rest of the inside, and they'd dragged the rocker over to Old Joe's place.

Anna and George followed the cook inside. "This here's where my baby lived?" asked Anna.

"Yes," the cook replied, "and she lived a good life here with old Aunty Mil. She was a good granny to your girl. Got her to sing in that sweet voice and everything."

Tears ran down Anna's face as she gripped George's arm. How bittersweet it felt to be in Janie's home. How close Anna felt to her daughter.

For the next week, Old Joe sat with George by the hour and instructed him on the details of the journey north the same way he had the Rubyhill Five. Anna listened to all the stories about Janie that anyone wanted to tell her. George slept and ate, ate and slept, slept and ate. The day he told Anna he felt restless, they both knew it was time to head north.

Just as they had a couple of weeks before, the former slaves of

Rubyhill gave a big send-off to the travelers. They sent them on their way with plenty of carrying food and the sounds of singing.

George squeezed Anna's hand as they walked down Rubyhill's drive. Anna squeezed back.

CHAPTER 9

Trouble

Nathan, Lucy, and Aleta were up and moving about when Janie and Maydean approached the maple grove. Janie saw that Blue was no longer thrashing or talking deliriously. He seemed to be in a deep sleep, his head resting on a big maple root. Janie wondered if Blue's deep sleep was a good thing or a bad thing.

Aleta stood quickly when she saw the two girls approach the grove. Janie could tell by Aleta's face and posture that she was nervous to see a white person. Now Lucy and Nathan stood, too, looking very concerned.

Janie spoke up right away. "This here's Maydean. She lives 'round here. She helped me find kindling. I want to boil us some apples, and I asked her if she's hungry."

This was quite a long speech coming from quiet Janie. The others stared at her, then at Maydean, then back at Janie. Bringing a white person to their encampment was absolutely the last thing they would expect any one of them to do. It was just too dangerous.

Janie understood the concern all too well. They'd been fortunate on the road so far. Nobody had really bothered them. Aleta prayed aloud for protection daily. Once they had stumbled upon a water moccasin while drawing water at a river, but it swam away without incident.

Even so, they would rather happen upon creatures of the out-doors than white strangers any day. Nothing good could come of letting white locals know the Rubyhill Five were traveling through.

But Janie's heart felt unusually light. Deep down, she knew it was good and right to offer this girl something to eat.

"Maydean, you any good at building fires?" she asked.

The white girl nodded and immediately started arranging kin-dling. Aleta continued to stare at Janie, a thousand unasked ques-tions in her eyes. Lucy and Nathan stood together and watched.

Janie ignored Aleta's probing looks. Instead she pulled out the boiling pot, took the paring knife, and began coring apples. She stopped when she realized that Maydean had stopped moving.

Maydean had just noticed the sleeping figure of Blue. "What's wrong with him?"

"He's got the fever," said Janie.

"Fever, huh." Maydean still didn't move. "You got to get him indoors."

Nobody responded to that. Obviously that was not a choice they had.

Maydeen looked at Janie, then Aleta, then back at Blue. "He can't come to my house 'cause my granddaddy hates your kind." She said this without emotion, then went on: "But there's a doctor over the hill apiece. He'd fix him. I can take you there."

"A white doctor?" asked Janie.

Maydean nodded. "He ain't like my granddaddy, though. Him and his wife used to hide your kind. I knew it, but I never told nobody." She scratched her head. "They take in everybody. Feed 'em good, too."

Janie looked at Aleta. They certainly could use a doctor for

Blue, and it sounded like this doctor might even treat black people. Maybe they should trust this girl all the way. Aleta shook her head and turned away.

But Janie felt strongly that Maydean was an answer to prayer. She grabbed Aleta's arm and pulled her away, out of earshot of the others.

"Aleta, we got to listen to her."

"Janie, you crazy? What you thinking? She's a white girl—and a mighty dirty one, at that."

"What's that got to do with anything? And I'm not crazy," Janie insisted. "Were we crazy when we took that rabbit from that white boy back then?"

Aleta shook her head. "But he was just one white person, and not a hateful one at that. The more white folks get wind of us here, the more trouble we get. 'Specially with one of us sick."

"She knows a doctor—"

"A white doctor," Aleta hissed, "and that ain't gonna do us no good. You know that."

Janie hissed right back. "If we don't get help for Blue, he gonna die right here."

Aleta's face fell. "I fear that, too, little sis. But if bringing in a whole lotta white people puts y'all in danger, too. . ." Her voice trailed off.

Janie could see the full weight of responsibility resting squarely on Aleta's shoulders. Together, Aleta and Blue could handle decisions for the five of them on this long, dangerous journey. Alone, it was a heavy load.

"Aleta," Janie said gently, "listen to me. I prayed 'bout this. I believe God sent this white girl to help us."

Aleta shook her head.

Janie continued. "Besides, she ain't got nothing. Look how she is. We got to share food with her. She even helped with the fire."

"It's not that," Aleta said. "If she'll sit and eat black folk's food, she's welcome to it. It's pulling in more whites that's got me nervous. No, little sis, we can't do no more than feed this girl."

Suddenly it started to snow. Hard. If they hadn't had to live in it, this snowfall would have been pretty. But big, wet snowflakes were coming down fast and furiously. They made no sound.

There was, however, one sound that reached Janie and Aleta from the maple grove—the sound of deep, hard coughing.

But it wasn't coming from Blue. Aleta and Janie looked at one another.

It was Lucy.

Kentucky

In a dry, warm barn in the middle of Kentucky, George and Anna took cover from a morning rainstorm. The sounds of rain on the rooftop made them drowsy, and before long, both of them snuggled down into the hay and fell asleep.

Janie came to Anna in a dream. Janie was still five years old. She looked into Anna's face with those huge, cinnamon-brown eyes of hers, and she began to sing. *Oh, what a beautiful sound,* thought Anna. *Sweet and high-pitched like a bird's.*

Suddenly a hawk swooped down and snatched the little girl away and up into the sky. Anna woke with a start. Trembling, she shook George awake.

"We got to pray right now. Janie's in trouble."

Without any question, George rose up. The two knelt in the hay and prayed throughout the rest of the storm. By the time the rain stopped, Anna felt calm, and she and George continued north on their journey to find their daughter.

CHAPTER 10

Mrs. Hull's Kitchen

Janie stood next to Maydean on the long front porch of a big, white farmhouse. She gazed around the farm itself. The many handsome barns were painted white, and the barnyards were so clean that to Janie they looked as if they'd been swept with a broom.

Most of the animals were apparently taking shelter from the storm, although a few horses stood outside with their backs to the driving snow. Janie hoped she could take shelter soon, too. Walking through this snowstorm had left the two girls cold and wet.

Maydean knocked on the front door of the farmhouse. After a moment, a white-haired woman opened it. She wore a black dress with a starched white collar and stood no taller than Janie.

The woman's rosy face beamed. "Good morning, dear Maydean. Come in out of the weather!"

The door opened wide, and Maydean stepped in. Janie paused. She'd never in her life walked into a white person's home through the front doorway.

The white woman smiled directly at Janie. "Come in, child, before thee catches thy death of cold."

What a strange way she talks. Janie stepped inside and quickly took in her surroundings. A polished staircase on the right side of the hallway climbed straight up to the second floor. A banister curved around at the top. Downstairs, framed portraits hung all over the walls of the hall. An oil lamp caused shadows to dance over the images.

Indoors, Janie felt instantly warmer. Then a wave of guilt swept over her as she remembered the others huddling under their snow-covered blankets in the maple grove.

"This here's Janie," said Maydean.

The white woman took Janie's cold hands and rubbed them in her own warm ones for a moment. This was even stranger to Janie. She had never in her life touched or been touched by a white person. "Oh, thee is so cold," the woman said. "Come into the kitchen. There is hot food on the stove. Come."

The two girls stomped the snow off their feet and onto a thick rug beside the door before following the woman straight down the central hallway. A closed door opened to a huge kitchen. The kitchen was even warmer than the hallway.

"Sit down, girls," said the woman. The two girls pulled sturdy chairs away from a large oak table and sat. The woman looked directly at Janie. "I am Mrs. Hull, Janie. I am pleased to make thy acquaintance."

Not knowing how to respond, Janie simply nodded, then looked at the floor, her hands in her lap. She felt shy in such a new and strange situation.

Maydean got to the heart of the matter. "Janie's people got caught in the snow in the maple grove on Uncle Willie's farm, Mrs. Hull. They come from down south, and they're headin' north. Some took sick—coughing fits and fever. They got to get inside."

Mrs. Hull looked instantly concerned. "How many?"

Maydean continued to speak for Janie. "Five all together, two of 'em sick."

"And how old is everyone, child?" Mrs. Hull spoke directly to Janie.

Janie cleared her throat. "Blue's seventeen, ma'am, and he's sick. The other sick one's Lucy, and she's ten. Nathan's ten, too. I'm eleven, and Aleta's seventeen." She stopped talking.

"Nobody elderly, then, and no babies?" Mrs. Hull said.

Janie shook her head.

"My husband will help them, child, and thee must not worry. Young people have a good chance of pulling through sickness of all kinds, and I'm sure thy long journey and the good Lord have made thee strong."

That sounded encouraging to Janie. Her toes were beginning to get warm. She could smell enticing odors in this kitchen. She looked around and spied chicken soup simmering on a back burner of a coal stove. The dregs of coffee were still warm and fragrant in a blue-speckled pot. Fresh baked bread sat on top of the sideboard. Janie's stomach growled out loud.

Mrs. Hull heard the stomach noises, and she smiled at Janie. "Thee is hungry."

"Yes, ma'am," Janie said. She quickly added, "But the others are out there in the snow. I can't eat when they can't." She stopped abruptly and looked down again. Had she been impolite? The words had just burst out of her.

But Mrs. Hull nodded vigorously. "Of course, child, I understand. I will fetch my husband immediately. That will take only a wee bit of time. While I do that, Maydean, please feed thyself and Janie, and please wrap food to take to the others. Get thy stomachs full and thy bodies warm so that both of thee are fortified for the outside."

Maydean hopped up and began fetching dishes from the sideboard. Janie surmised that perhaps this cozy, orderly farmhouse was Maydean's safe place from her drunken granddaddy. Janie felt better for Maydean.

She felt better about her own situation, too. It looked like help was surely on its way. *Thank You, Lord.*

Mrs. Hull pulled on a heavy black cloak and wool bonnet. Once more, she spoke to Janie directly. "Child," she said kindly, "thee must not fret. My husband is an excellent physician and will help the sick ones. Until I locate him in the barns, of course, we cannot leave. In the meantime, thee must take nourishment while I am gone. That is best for all concerned. Does thee understand?"

Janie nodded. "Thank you, ma'am."

Mrs. Hull left the room, and soon they heard the back door open and close. A draft of cold flashed through the warm kitchen.

Maydean ladled up a steaming bowl of soup and placed it with a spoon in front of Janie. "Eat," she said. She moved to the sideboard and cut two thick slices of bread and placed them right on the table next to the soup. Then she helped herself to the soup pot.

Janie waited. Should she eat—or not? The others back in the maple grove were cold and wet and hungry. . . .

"Eat, Janie," Maydean said again, as if reading her mind. "Mrs. Hull's right. We got to get warmed up while we wait. Then we can do better outside."

Janie nodded. She said a silent grace, picked up her spoon, and dug in.

CHAPTER 11

To the Rescue

Mrs. Hull was true to her word. By the time Janie had devoured her bowl of soup and a slice of bread with butter, Mrs. Hull had returned with her husband in tow.

"Janie, this is Dr. Hull." A short man with twinkling eyes nodded at Janie and Maydean. He was a powerfully built man in spite of his white hair, and he wore good wool clothing. Janie noted that his black clothes were clean, even though he'd just come in from farm work. He carried the good odor of fresh air.

Dr. Hull fished a large black valise out from under a worktable. "Virginia, dear, I'll hook up the team and bring the sleigh around front. Please give the young ladies as many blankets as they can carry."

"Yes, Otto," Mrs. Hull said, and she hurried into the room off the kitchen while the doctor headed for the back door.

Maydean had eaten quickly. Now she hopped to her feet, and Janie watched her spread two slices of bread with butter and wrap them in newspaper. "Only two of your friends gonna eat, I'll wager," she said. Then she put on her jacket and stuffed the food into her pockets. "Come on, Janie. Dr. Hull's gonna be ready in no time."

Mrs. Hull called to them from the side room. They found her in a storage room full of linens, pillows, and blankets. Janie had not seen so many linens since Rubyhill's Big House before the war. Mrs. Hull loaded both girls down with heavy blankets and quilts, then led the way to the front door.

Before long, a team of two large, black draft horses pulled a long vehicle up to the porch. Janie had never seen such a thing as this sleigh. It looked like a passenger wagon, long with three wide bench seats, but it sat on runners instead of wheels. It was so big she could understand why two horses were needed to pull it. Dr. Hull occupied the driver's seat.

Blankets and girls were loaded onto the sleigh. Dr. Hull bundled each girl in an extra blanket, waved to Mrs. Hull, and started the huge horses down the snowy drive. Janie barely blinked, it all happened so fast.

Maydean called out directions to Dr. Hull. The sleigh was able to move quickly over the accumulating snow. Within ten minutes, they arrived at the maple grove.

Janie looked quickly for her friends. Finally she saw the pile of snow-covered blankets with Nathan and Aleta peering out from under. As she drew closer, Janie noted fear in their eyes.

Janie watched Aleta scrutinize the situation of a white man coming for them in a horse-drawn sleigh. Aleta frowned, but when she saw Janie wave at her from behind Dr. Hull, she stopped frowning.

Without further ado, Aleta sprang into action. She gathered the dry blankets offered her and wrapped them around Lucy and Blue, who both lay still. She helped Nathan brush the wet snow off himself, then dried herself off. Janie jumped out of the sleigh, gathered all their gear, and threw it into the back of the sleigh.

Dr. Hull introduced himself to Aleta, then made a quick assessment of the sick youths. He took off one glove and pressed his fingers to each of their necks. He ran his bare hand over their fever-ish faces. He lifted their eyelids and looked at their eyes. Then he bodily picked up Blue and placed him in the sleigh. He stepped back and did the same with Lucy; then he tucked blankets around their deeply sleeping forms.

Janie's jaw dropped at the white man's strength and quick agil-ity. He was a farmer, of course, used to hauling and lifting. But to Janie, he seemed kind of old for such strength. Of course Lucy didn't weigh much, and Blue had dropped weight in the past couple weeks. Still, Dr. Hull surely was a strong man.

Before long, the sleigh was loaded with people, and Maydean handed out the buttered bread. Dr. Hull slapped the reins, and off they went into the snow, the runners hissing as they traveled over the ground. Their return to the Hull farm was slowed only a little by the extra weight.

Once they arrived at the farm and unloaded the wagon, much to Janie's surprise, Mrs. Hull said there were beds ready upstairs for Janie, Aleta, and Nathan. She also had made up beds for Blue and Lucy in two back rooms on the first floor. "Dr. Hull and I sleep downstairs," she explained, "and we must be close to these two tonight. When they are well, they will move upstairs."

Janie and Aleta looked at each other quickly. *A white woman wants us to sleep in her house?*

Aleta offered to help Mrs. Hull with Blue and Lucy, but the older woman refused. "Thee must get into dry clothes, dear. Betsy will bring up warm water and towels so thee can bathe. We have clothes in the wardrobes upstairs, and something will fit. Betsy will help thee look."

A smiling young woman with blond braids pinned up appeared

in the doorway. She wore an apron over her calico dress. "I'm Betsy. Come on upstairs."

Mrs. Hull added one more thing. "We shall eat supper in an hour, and afterward I shall expect all of thee to take thy rest for as long as thee can. Thy friends are in Dr. Hull's capable hands and God's, as well."

Maydean moved to the kitchen while the others followed Betsy up the steep stairs. Aleta and Janie would share a big, four-poster bed in a large room in the front part of the upstairs. A smaller trundle bed was tucked underneath the high bed. Across the hall, Nathan would sleep on one of two single beds.

Each bed was made up with flannel sheets, warm quilts, and pillows—truly a new experience for the young former slaves. None of them had ever slept in such luxury. None of them had ever slept in a bed. None had even slept in an actual house before now.

Just as Mrs. Hull had predicted, the wardrobes held clean clothes that fit all three young people. Betsy chatted away as she handed out dresses, pants, shirts, nightgowns, and warm socks.

"Before the war, slaves escaping to the north stayed here, so Mrs. Hull always had good clothes on hand for them to wear in their new life," she said. "Sometimes they stayed a long time gaining their health before moving on. Dr. Hull is a gifted doctor. And Mrs. Hull is a wonderful nurse."

Nathan piped up. "Why do they talk that way?"

"They're Quakers," Betsy explained. "That's the way they talk. They believe it's a way of treating everyone equally under God."

"Aren't you their daughter?" asked Nathan.

"I'm a distant cousin—from the Methodist side of the family." Betsy laughed. "I work here for room and board and some money, which I'm saving. I plan to move to Detroit, Michigan, next year to attend teachers' college."

Janie felt a twinge of envy. How smart this young woman must be. And so kind. What a good teacher she would make. Janie noticed Aleta eyeing the young woman with approval as well. The two were about the same age.

"So now, does everyone have towels and dry clothes?" asked Betsy. "And nightclothes, too?" Of course Betsy couldn't know that the Rubyhill youths had never slept in nightclothes, only in their day clothes. And they never told her. They simply nodded gratefully.

"Fine, then. I'm going downstairs. During cold weather, we eat in the kitchen, so come there when you're ready." She smiled once more and headed downstairs.

Janie and Aleta looked at each other. They were too exhausted to say much. Besides, Nathan had been talking for everyone ever since they got to the Hull farm.

"Did you see them horses? They moved through that snow like it was shallow water. Big healthy animals, too. What was that thing we rode in? It was so fast! Look at these pillows! Beds look so good, I may jus' sleep all day. Food smells good, too. Cain't wait to eat. . ."

And on and on. Finally Aleta shushed him and sent him to get ready in his own room.

Aleta was quiet at first as they washed at the basins of soapy water. Finally she spoke. "Janie, I sure am thankful you were listening to the Lord this morning. I don't know where we'd be. I don't know if any of us woulda lived 'til morning. I don't know. . . ." Aleta stopped and sighed.

Janie reached over and squeezed her friend's hand. "I'm thankful, too. These are nice people. And so's Maydean."

Aleta shook her head slowly. "I was wrong about her."

"How were you supposed to know?" asked Janie. "She looks a fright." Janie shrugged. "And she's white."

"Still no excuse to think the evil thoughts I was having," said Aleta. She pulled on a blue wool dress and a white pinafore apron over it. "Oh, this feels so good. Thank You, Jesus."

Janie dressed quickly in the warm dry clothes Betsy had laid out for her. "Ready to go downstairs?"

"I sure am, little sis."

In the kitchen, the large oak table was set. There was a place for everyone who could sit and eat—Dr. and Mrs. Hull, Betsy, Aleta, Nathan, Janie, and Maydean, who had washed her hands and face, Janie noticed. Janie could see now that the girl had freckles.

Betsy placed a large, lovely serving dish of piping hot chicken stew on the table. The stew was loaded with carrots, potatoes, and onions. Mrs. Hull sliced bread on a wooden board.

As the supper table was being made ready, Dr. Hull filled everyone in on how the patients were. He kept it brief. "They both have fevers. We shall stay up with them, as fevers have the habit of rising at night. We will know more by morning. In the meantime, let us pray for thy friends."

Dr. Hull bowed his head and said grace, adding special prayers for Blue and Lucy. After the "amen," Janie glanced at Aleta. Janie realized once again the burden Aleta had carried all day and all the night before. Aleta's relief was clear. Having these kind people take that burden and carry it for now was a godsend.

At first, Aleta and Nathan stared at their dishes of bread and stew without touching any of it. This was the first hot meal they'd seen in weeks. But their awe did not last long. Soon both were devouring the delicious supper along with everyone else.

Mrs. Hull and Betsy replenished the food throughout the meal, and the youths—including Maydean—ate until they were satisfied. Even then, they mopped their plates clean with their bread crusts.

Now Janie's stomach was so full that it made her extremely sleepy. As the Hulls and Betsy talked, Janie caught herself nodding off. She jerked her head up and made herself keep her eyes open. That's when she saw that both Aleta and Nathan had fallen sound asleep in their chairs.

Mrs. Hull smiled at her husband. He nodded and rose. The strong man picked Nathan right up off his chair and carried him upstairs. Betsy and Mrs. Hull pulled Aleta to her feet and helped her up the stairs. Janie managed to bid Maydean good night and get herself up the stairs, too, holding onto the banister the whole sleepy way.

In their bedroom, Janie and Aleta struggled into flannel nightgowns and fell into bed. Aleta rose up once more to put out the lamp, and the two girls were asleep within minutes.

It would be a long time before the Rubyhill Five traveled again.

CHAPTER 12

Wintering

"Janie, what you got there?"

Maydean pointed to the bodice of Janie's dress. It had become a bit of a nervous habit for Janie to trace the outline of that dangling cross through the fabric of her clothes. Since arriving at the Hulls, Aleta had frowned gently at Janie every time she saw her do it. But Aleta wasn't in the room right now.

Janie pulled out the cross. "Nathan found this buried with Miz Laura's silver, back at Rubyhill. Miz Laura told us to take whatever we wanted, so Nathan gave me this."

Maydean's blue eyes twinkled. "That makes Nathan your beau."

"What's a beau?" asked Janie.

Maydean tossed her red mane of hair and grinned. "Somebody who's sweet on you."

Janie shook her head. "No, Nathan's like a brother."

The two girls sat cross-legged on the braided rug next to a crackling fire in the front-room fireplace. The snow that had brought the Rubyhill Five to the Hull farmhouse had stopped, leaving behind a world of white. Maydean had gone home after supper the previous night but returned through the snow in the morning. She had joined them all for hot oatmeal, and Mrs. Hull had invited her to spend the day.

The house had been quiet since breakfast. Mrs. Hull reported that Dr. Hull was in the back bedrooms, tending to Blue and Lucy. She said he would speak to everyone about it later.

Maydean reached out and gently touched the cross. "Can I look at it?" she asked.

Janie nodded. She took the chain off and handed it to the red-head. Maydean turned the pewter cross over in her hand. "What's it say here on the back?"

"You can't read?" Janie blurted out. She thought all white people could read.

A dark cloud seemed to spread across Maydean's freckled face. She shook her head. She seemed embarrassed.

"I'm sorry, Maydean," Janie said quickly. "I don't know no black folks who can read, that's for sure. But I just figured all white folks could." She paused. "That wasn't too smart of me."

"My granddaddy won't let me go to school," Maydean said. "And he can't read hisself." She stopped talking. After a short uncomfortable silence, Maydean handed the cross back. "It's real pretty, Janie," she said.

"Thanks, Maydean," said Janie. "You know," she added, "your name's real pretty, too."

Maydean's face lit up. "You think so?"

Janie nodded. "I never heard the name before."

"I'm named for my mommy and daddy—May and Dean, see?"

"How come you live with your granddaddy and not with them?" asked Janie.

The cloud came back to Maydean's face. "They's both dead."

It seemed Janie was bringing up difficult subjects for Maydean today. She said no more.

But a memory nudged her until it came full into the light. Suddenly Janie remembered something she'd forgotten for many years. "Oh my," she said aloud.

"What?" asked Maydean.

"I just recollected my momma telling me my name used to be Georgeanna. I was named after my poppa and her, too—George and Anna." Janie sat and let the memory sink in. "Georgeanna," she said again.

"That's real pretty. How's come you're called Janie then?" asked Maydean.

Janie thought hard until the reason finally surfaced. "I recollect what Momma said now. Master's wife said Georgeanna was too fine a name for a black baby. She's the one that named me Janie."

Maydean stared at Janie for a moment. "How come she did that if you wasn't her baby?"

"That's how it was in those days," Janie said. She looked at her new friend. "My momma didn't have no choice, Maydean. We was slaves."

The look Maydean gave Janie showed that Maydean had no clue what she was talking about. Janie wondered if maybe Maydean didn't realize what a slave was. Who did Maydean think the Hulls had been hiding all those years?

All Maydean said was, "You like being called Janie?"

Janie shrugged. "Never been called nothin' else."

A heavy curtain in the doorway was pulled aside, and Betsy stuck her head in. "Girls, come to the kitchen. Dr. Hull has some news."

The Hull kitchen was always so wonderfully warm that Janie loved simply walking into it. At the table sat Aleta, Nathan, and

Dr. Hull. Mrs. Hull and Betsy scurried about making tea and scraping hot gingerbread out of a black skillet. Janie loved that part of being in the kitchen, too—the delicious, plentiful food. She and Maydean slid onto chairs and waited.

Dr. Hull cleared his throat. "Good morning, everyone. I know all of thee must be worried about Blue and Lucy. Mrs. Hull and I tended to them throughout the night. The worst is over for young Blue; his fever broke as the sun came up." The doctor paused. "Little Lucy is still in a bad way, I'm afraid. I suspect all of thee have lacked good nourishment for some time now, and that has weakened Lucy considerably. She has little to fight with."

Will Lucy die? The thought took hold inside Janie, and she was instantly sick to her stomach. She looked quickly at Nathan. Lucy was his twin, the only blood family he remembered having. Understandably, Nathan was fighting back tears.

Mrs. Hull turned from the sideboard and spoke in her kind tone. "Dr. Hull and I are surprised that not all of thee fell ill the same way as Lucy and Blue, but we feel certain that possibility has passed. Praise God the fever did not spread further." She looked at each brown face at the table. "Dr. Hull and I want to invite thee to stay with us through the winter to rest and fortify thy bodies for the journey to Chicago. Will thee stay with us? Until spring?"

Numbly, all three Rubyhill youths nodded as one.

"Good," she said. She turned back to her tasks.

"The more fortunate news for Lucy," said Dr. Hull, "is that sometimes youths can handle a great deal more illness than adults. Lucy is ten, yes?"

"We'll be eleven soon, sir," said Nathan in a tiny voice.

Dr. Hull looked at Nathan a moment, then reached over and

patted his shoulder. "Son, I assure thee that Mrs. Hull and I will do all we can to help thy sister pull through. In the meantime, let us all pray for Lucy's recovery."

With that, Dr. Hull lowered his head and began to pray aloud for Lucy's survival, as well as for the continued recovery of Blue. Then he excused himself and returned to his patients.

Except for the bustling noises Mrs. Hull and Betsy made, the kitchen was silent. Then Mrs. Hull sat down at the table.

"While thee young ones are with us," she said, "Betsy and I shall teach thee in the mornings. We shall meet here at the kitchen table."

Nathan looked up. "Teach us what, ma'am?"

Mrs. Hull smiled gently. "To read, young man. And to do arithmetic. How does that sound?"

Nathan slowly began to smile. Janie felt thrilled. She looked at Aleta, whose face once again wore a look of profound relief. Reading and working with numbers were skills they all knew they needed for the future in Chicago.

Betsy spoke up. "Mrs. Hull will teach you arithmetic, and I will teach you to read. Frankly, I will appreciate the opportunity to try my hand at actually teaching. I need the practice, so you'll be helping me as much as I hope to help you."

Janie looked at Maydean, but she could not read her facial expression. Should she ask if Maydean could join them? Would that embarrass Maydean, she being white? Janie decided to say nothing now but to approach Mrs. Hull about it later.

Betsy placed a plate of gingerbread squares on the table and poured glasses of fresh milk for all. Then she poured herself a cup of tea and sat down next to Janie.

"Miss Betsy," Janie whispered.

The blond girl looked at her.

Janie pulled the cross out of her dress and lifted it from around her neck. "What does this say?" She handed the cross and its chain to Betsy.

Betsy fingered the cross, smiled, and whispered back, "It says, 'Make a joyful noise.' It's from the Bible." She reached over and draped the chain back around Janie's neck.

Janie turned the phrase over in her mind. *Make a joyful noise.* The mystery was solved.

How she wished she could tell Aunty Mil.

Kentucky

An early November ice storm hit Kentucky as George and Anna traveled across the state. As a result, they found themselves spending the night on a horse farm near Lexington. They had made good time in spite of oddly frequent snow squalls, but they were not prepared for ice.

Nor was either of them really prepared for the hardship of the road. George's strength was not fully back, and neither of them were used to such cold. They weren't feeling very young anymore. Both of them were bone weary. Their love for their daughter had kept George and Anna moving northward, but it was starting to make sense to get off the road for winter and start up again in spring.

Good with horses since his days at Shannon Oaks, George sought employment at the Lexington stables of Mr. Albert DuPont.

He was hired on the spot. The job provided a room over the horses, and Anna was allowed to stay, as well.

Since Mr. DuPont was a widower, Anna approached him with the offer to use her sewing and knitting skills to get him and his hired men ready for winter. A sensible man, DuPont happily hired Anna also.

So George and Anna decided they should spend the winter at DuPont Acres, put their money away, and start out again in spring. "We can take a train then, sugar," George promised. "We'll get to Chicago fast and in style."

Anna laughed. To her "in style" would simply mean staying clean and not sleeping out in the weather. And that sounded just fine to her. Initially, she was reluctant not to keep moving, but she saw the wisdom of shoring up their strength, earning money, and looking less bedraggled when they hit the sophisticated city of Chicago.

Besides, the recent nightmare about Janie had not returned. Anna felt a peace about her little girl, a peace for which she was grateful.

CHAPTER 13

Change in the Air

"Mrs. Hull?" Janie looked over the banister and spied the mistress of the house at the foot of the stairs. The white-haired woman looked up and beamed at Janie.

"And how was thy rest last night, Janie?" This was Janie's second day at the Hull farm.

Janie ran lightly down the stairs. "Very good, ma'am, thank you." She joined the woman in the hallway. Mrs. Hull was so short that Janie could look her straight in the eyes. "Mrs. Hull, did you know Maydean can't read?"

Mrs. Hull's mouth opened in surprise. "No, child, I did not know this. Why, there's a school not far from her house, and I assumed. . ." She looked down for a moment, then back at Janie. "Is thee quite certain of this, child?"

"Yes, ma'am. Maydean told me herself. Her granddaddy won't let her go to school."

"Oh, I see." Mrs. Hull frowned. "Well, then, it is good of thee to bring it up. We should do what we can about that, shouldn't we, young Janie? Let us see if dear Maydean would like to join our little kitchen-table school. How does that sound?"

"That sounds real fine, ma'am," said Janie. She and Mrs. Hull smiled at each other.

"Now, dear Janie, I have a surprise. Come with me." Mrs. Hull led the way to the kitchen.

Indeed, the warm kitchen held the most wonderful surprise. Sitting at the table was the very thin figure of Blue, sipping from a cup of tea. In front of him sat a small dish of stewed pears. Blue's gaunt face made his eyes look big as saucers. Aleta sat next to him, her eyes never leaving his face.

Seeing Blue sitting up and handling that dainty flowered cup made tears well in Janie's eyes. "Blue!" she called.

Blue looked up at Janie and grinned weakly. "Hey, girl. Come sit down here and help me eat them pears." His hand shook as he lowered the teacup. It rattled softly in its saucer.

Janie slid into the chair next to Blue. "Them pears is yours, Blue. You got to eat 'em."

"That's what I been telling him," Aleta fussed. "He's got to eat. That fever took the stuffin' right out of him."

Blue laughed softly. He placed his hand on Aleta's and left it there a moment. Aleta's face flushed, and her brown eyes sparkled.

Janie was surprised. She'd thought of them all as brothers and sisters, but clearly Blue and Aleta were—what had Maydean called it? Janie thought a minute. Oh yes—they were beaus. Sweet on each other. It looked that way to Janie, anyway.

Change in the air. Aunty Mil's favorite phrase drifted through Janie's mind. *Yes,* Janie thought, *lots of change in the air.*

Aleta pulled her hand away from Blue and looked self-consciously at Janie. "Blue's gonna be here at our kitchen school. He's gonna learn to read, too. Mrs. Hull says he can sit up for an hour at a time. Won't be long 'til we start our lessons."

"That's good," said Janie. She paused. "How's Lucy?"

"Nobody's saying nothing," said Aleta. "Dr. Hull's in there with her now. We got to keep prayin', little sis."

Blue looked at the tablecloth. It was hard to read his face. He most likely knew he had almost died, and he must be very worried for Lucy. Janie breathed a quick, silent prayer.

The kitchen door to the hall opened, and in walked Maydean and Betsy. They stopped at the sight of Blue.

Aleta introduced everyone who hadn't met, and Blue thanked Maydean for taking them to Hull Farm.

"I'm awful glad you're better," Maydean said. "Mrs. Hull will feed you good—I can tell you that." She turned to Janie. "Betsy's gonna braid my hair. You wanna come watch?"

Janie looked at Maydean's matted red mane. It would need a lot done to it before braiding would even be possible. Betsy certainly had her work cut out for her.

Janie glanced over at Blue. He and Aleta were looking shyly at one another again. Janie smiled inside. She hadn't seen that coming—Blue and Aleta together—but it made so much sense. They were meant to be together.

"Sure, Maydean," Janie said. "I'll come along."

The three girls headed into the front room, where the morning fire burned warm and slow. Maydean still wore men's pants, and she plopped down on the rug in front of the fire. She sat cross-legged, and Betsy sank down behind her. "What a marvelous head of hair you have, Maydean," Betsy said.

Janie thought that was a very kind thing to say. The fact of the matter was Maydean's long, curly hair was dirty and matted.

But Betsy didn't seem to mind. She brushed and brushed Maydean's hair. She worked oil through the matting with her fingers until she could brush every snarl free. Then she brushed some more.

Janie thought about Aunty Mil and how she used to comb Janie's nappy hair with only those long fingers of hers, then braid it nice and snug. Whenever Aunty Mil hit a snarl and had to work through it with her fingers, she would coo, "Little girl, you got the patience of Job."

The first time Aunty Mil had said this, little Janie had piped up, "How come you say that?"

" 'Cause you let Aunty Mil pull on this knot of hair, and you don't complain or cry or nothin'."

"Who's Job?" Janie had asked.

"A patient man o' God," was all Aunty said. But the next time— and every time—she untangled a snarl, she said, "Little girl, you got the patience of Job." Janie came to expect it and like it. Those hair sessions were some of the fondest memories Janie had.

It took a long time for Betsy to get Maydean's hair unsnarled. Throughout what had to be a painful process, Maydean simply sat quietly and looked straight ahead into the fire. She reminded Janie of the horses back in Georgia, how they looked when the grooms-men brushed their sleek coats. Those big creatures always stood perfectly still, looked straight ahead, and seemed to like how the brushing felt. That's how Maydean looked to Janie.

Before long, Janie could see that Betsy was right—Maydean did indeed have a glorious mane of hair. Now Betsy's fingers worked and worked some more until she'd braided two long, thick braids, snugly woven to stay put.

"Voilà!" said Betsy.

"What's that mean?" asked Maydean.

"It means I'm done, and you are beautiful. Turn around so Janie can see."

Maydean squirmed on the rug until she faced Janie.

"Oh, Maydean," Janie said, "you got to look in a mirror. You look so pretty."

Betsy pulled Maydean to her feet, moved her to the gilded mirror across the room, and placed her square in front of it. Janie watched Maydean's reflection. The redhead's jaw dropped.

"That's me?" she asked.

Betsy nodded. "I can help you keep it that way, too. I'm giving you this hairbrush to take home, and. . ."

Maydean's expression changed. "If it's all right, Miss Betsy, can I leave the brush here and just use it here?" Maydean's eyes looked anxious. "If I take it home, I might lose it."

Without a question, Betsy nodded. "Of course. I will find a special spot for it, Maydean. It will be your personal grooming spot in this house."

Maydean's shoulders drooped visibly. "Thank you, Miss Betsy," was all she said.

Mrs. Hull stuck her head in the room. "Girls, Dr. Hull wants to see us." Her eyes widened when she saw Maydean. "Why, look at that! How lovely thee looks, my dear." Then she hurried to the kitchen.

Everyone immediately gathered in the kitchen again—all except Blue, who was resting in his room, and Lucy, of course. Aleta, Janie, Nathan, Mrs. Hull, Betsy, and Maydean waited expectantly for news.

Dr. Hull was brief. "I want thee all to know," he began, "that in this past hour, our young Lucy's fever has broken." He looked at each of them. "She is still unwell. I do not know if any permanent harm has come from her days of fever, and I shan't know for a while. We must continue to pray for the child's health."

With that, Dr. Hull led a short, heartfelt prayer, then returned to the back of the house.

It happened so fast that nobody said anything for a bit. Then Mrs. Hull spoke briskly. "I believe it is time to start our school. Betsy and I can give Lucy any special help she needs while she's recovering, and before long, she'll be caught up. Let us begin in the morning."

The Rubyhill youths nodded.

Mrs. Hull looked at Maydean. "Will thee be joining us as well, dear?"

Maydean looked at her hands. She shrugged.

"I shall take that as a yes," Mrs. Hull simply said. "Now Betsy and I shall see all of thee bright and early tomorrow after breakfast. We'll meet right here at the table."

With that, Mrs. Hull left to join the doctor at Lucy's side.

Aleta turned to Maydean. "You got the most beautiful hair," Aleta said.

Maydean simply squirmed in her chair and grinned.

CHAPTER 14

Christmas Eve

A rooster woke Janie up on the morning of Christmas Eve. She looked out the bedroom window to find the hills and fields covered in another heavy blanket of fresh snow and tinged with the pink of a soon-to-rise sun.

Janie sat up and hugged her knees under the warm, heavy quilts. Aleta was already up and out of the room, probably downstairs helping. The Rubyhill youths who had not taken sick offered to do any work they could at the Hull farm, and their help was appreciated.

Janie smiled. She felt happy these days, more content than she had been since Aunty Mil was alive and more hopeful for the future than she'd ever been in her whole life.

There were many blessings for Janie to count as she stayed snuggled under the quilts. First of all, Lucy was getting stronger every day. She would eventually move upstairs to Aleta and Janie's room, but right now the stairs were a bit too much for the very weakened Lucy. Dr. Hull said that he couldn't see anything deeply wrong with Lucy from the long fever, but he warned them that she would be quieter than she had been before being sick. That would last a long time, he said, most likely all winter.

Indeed, Janie found Lucy to be very subdued. She sat quietly at the kitchen table with everyone for meals and for short periods of schooling. Sometimes Janie caught Lucy watching her move about the room. Lucy's big dark eyes were expressionless until Janie made a funny face. Then Lucy's eyes smiled, but often her face did not.

"You all right, Lucy?" Janie would ask.

Lucy would nod and continue to watch Janie with those big dark eyes. After a while, Janie understood that Lucy had simply lost all her energy at those times and that watching the others was entertainment for the still-weak girl. When this happened, Janie would help her friend back to her room in the back of the house. Lucy would crawl into bed and fall asleep almost instantly. This happened every day, but the naps were getting shorter every day, too.

Of course, people had gotten sick before in Janie's world, but they usually got better faster than this. Janie sorely missed Lucy's friendship. Maydean was turning into a friend, but Lucy had been Janie's friend for many years. Aleta seemed preoccupied with Blue these days, and Janie didn't feel she should take up Aleta's time. And Nathan. . .well, Nathan was a boy.

At least Janie could see the baby steps Lucy's health was taking. And they were forward steps. She would be her old self soon enough.

On the other hand, Blue was back to his full strength and former sassiness. He and Nathan helped Dr. Hull and some hired hands with the farm work. Blue had early on returned to teasing Janie like a big brother, and everyone was relieved to see it.

And then there was the Blue and Aleta romance. It took a couple of weeks for Janie to adjust, but now she found herself happy to see how Blue acted with Aleta. He did not treat her as a sister anymore at all. He held Aleta's hand under the table, and he watched her cross a room as if nobody else were in the room with them. Janie figured that must be what love between a boy and a girl looked like.

These winter days found Aleta making a handsome quilt. She allowed Janie to help her with it. Lucy was too weary to concentrate on needlework, but she sat with them. Maydean had no interest in it. She preferred to help out with the chickens and cows outdoors or work in the kitchen on occasion with Betsy.

Maydean had truly blossomed from the dirt-caked, wild-haired girl Janie had met weeks ago. Maydean spent almost every day at the Hull farm. Janie watched the girl transform from dirty to clean, from what Blue called "half boy" to all girl. Maydean still wore men's clothing, but now Janie knew why. That was all her drunken granddaddy had for her to wear, and she didn't want him to wonder where she got new clothes.

Janie had also learned why the frightening man did not allow his granddaughter to go to school. "It's 'cause he cain't read," Maydean finally told her, "and he can't have nobody smarter'n him around. If he knew I could read, he'd beat the smartness right out of me."

Janie was horrified to hear this, but she said nothing else about it to Maydean. The Hull farmhouse door was always open to the child, so she had a sanctuary. She kept her books at the Hull farm along with the hairbrush and combs Betsy gave her. Maydean kept her hair braided, but she never worked on it at her own house, only at the Hull's. And every evening before dark, Maydean trudged on back to her grandfather's house. Now that Janie understood all that, it was an even happier thing to have Maydean around.

The Rubyhill Five's new reality still took some getting used to. All five of them now spent time each day with—even ate with—white folks. The strangeness of it never completely went away during their winter at the Hull farm. But Janie and the others had grown to love the Hulls, Betsy, and Maydean.

Mrs. Hull's and Betsy's good cooking filled out hollow cheeks and skinny arms. All the Rubyhill Five gained weight and soon looked hale and hearty. Even Maydean was no longer so thin, and her cheeks were rosy all the time. Janie appreciated not going to bed hungry. Every night she thanked the Lord for that.

Best of all, Janie and her friends could read. It had not taken long. Betsy said that they not only were more than ready to learn new things, they were also all very smart. The group progressed quickly under the kind and careful instruction of Mrs. Hull and Betsy.

Soon they could both read and perform tasks of basic arithmetic. Janie found she was particularly good at this, and it was fun for her. She now was learning multiplication tables and even fractions.

The young students also took lessons in proper spoken grammar. At first, none of them had been particularly interested in talking in any other way but their own. Deep down inside, they also didn't want to speak like a Yankee. Such ideas had been part of their rural southern upbringing, though they never spoke any of those ideas aloud at the kitchen table.

But Betsy, who came from St. Louis, told them, "You're eventually moving to Chicago. If you don't change how you speak, the good citizens of Chicago will dismiss you as country bumpkins. Let me help you so that northern people treat you with respect when they hear you speak."

Of course, Maydean wasn't going to Chicago, but she was most excited about learning proper grammar. She confided to Janie that she was formulating a plan. "What I want to do now, see, is to be a teacher like Betsy. I'm talkin' to her 'bout it all the time in the kitchen. She says I can get caught up real quick. She thinks I can do it." Janie noticed that Maydean's face brightened with passionate energy when she spoke like this.

Another exciting benefit the Rubyhill Five and Maydean had during kitchen school was that now they could all read the Bible. Slaves had almost no access to the Bible since they were not allowed to read nor gather for church. Janie was stunned at how much was in just one book.

At first it was difficult with all the old-fashioned language and complicated sentences. But Mrs. Hull and Betsy patiently walked them through the hard words to understand the thrilling stories of the Old Testament and the birth, life, and death of Jesus in the New Testament.

Now Janie knew where to find, "Make a joyful noise." She also knew that the Lord considered her singing such joyful noise.

Janie learned who Job was, the man Aunty Mil said had patience. That Old Testament hero had lost everything, and in some ways, Janie felt like him. But through it all, she read, he still loved the good Lord. Janie considered her own losses, and she came to see that all people went through pain in life, no matter who they were. Janie determined that no matter what, she would continue her love and dependence on the Lord.

There were two exciting things Janie thought about this snowy morning. One was that her birthday was tomorrow on Christmas Day.

The other exciting thing had to do with reading. Mrs. Hull had told them that on Christmas morning they would be reading aloud the story of baby Jesus as found in the Gospel of Luke. "We shall gather around the dining-room table, and thee shall take turns with the scripture verses," she said. "Dr. Hull and I shared the reading of the Christmas story with our own children, and we would feel privileged to do the same with all of thee."

At first nobody spoke. Then Mrs. Hull laughed gently. "Do not fear, young ones—we shall all share the difficult words!"

Of course, they had planned a succulent dinner, as well. A turkey stuffed with dressing would be roasting in the big black oven long before breakfast. Betsy and Maydean had been baking all week for the feast.

Janie had heard Mrs. Hull invite Maydean to come celebrate Christmas with them if her grandfather didn't mind. "It's just another day to him, ma'am," Maydean responded matter-of-factly. "I'll be here. Thank you, ma'am."

All these things turned over in Janie's mind as she watched the rising sun begin to color the fields a deep gold. She kicked back the quilt and gingerly slid to the floor. The wood planks were always so cold to her bare feet that she immediately hopped to the big rag rug a few feet away. There, Janie hopped from one foot to the other to get dressed. She still wore the pewter cross around her neck, and it bumped comfortably under her clothes as she hopped around.

Once dressed, Janie bounded down the stairs to the kitchen. Mrs. Hull turned from the stove. "Good morning, Janie. Thee is hungry?"

"Yes, ma'am, I am." A piping bowl of oatmeal was set in front of her, followed by a glass of milk. Janie bowed her head and silently said grace. She opened her eyes, took a deep breath, and smiled.

"Thee is happy this morning," Mrs. Hull observed.

Janie nodded. "Tomorrow's my birthday," she blurted out.

Mrs. Hull turned to face Janie. "Really, child? On Christmas Day?"

Janie grinned and nodded vigorously.

"Well, this is cause for celebration." Mrs. Hull sat down. "How is it that thee knows when thy birthday is, child?"

"Slaves didn't work on Christmas, ma'am."

Mrs. Hull's face made a quick flinch. "Ah," she said smoothly, "I see. How convenient to have been born on a day one can remember!"

Janie nodded again and poured corn syrup on her oatmeal.

"Does thee know the birthdays of thy friends, Janie?"

Janie stopped with her spoon in midair. Never had she even wondered about the birthdays of Aleta, Blue, or the twins. She simply accepted that they did not know. She always felt special, in fact, that she knew her own.

Janie set her spoon down. She looked at the tablecloth. "No, ma'am," she said softly, "I don't know their birthdays. The only birthday I've ever known is mine." Somehow it sounded selfish when she said it out loud.

Mrs. Hull looked at Janie thoughtfully. "And does thee think it matters to them?"

Janie pondered that for a moment. "I think it matters to Lucy and Nathan, 'cause they's twins."

"They *are* twins," Mrs. Hull gently corrected her.

"Yes, ma'am, that's what I meant. They have each other, blood and all, but that's all they know."

"What about Blue and Aleta?"

"I never heard them say nothin'—anything about it, ma'am."

"How old will thee be tomorrow, Janie?"

"Twelve, ma'am."

"We shall celebrate, young Janie." Mrs. Hull gave her a rosy-cheeked smile. "A birthday is a special thing. And to celebrate thy birthday on the same day we celebrate the birth of our Lord Jesus is special indeed." She stood and turned back to the stove.

An idea came to Janie. The twins knew they had been born in winter. Couldn't they share Janie's birthday with her? Couldn't they simply decide that was their birthday, too? They could all turn one year older together. They could celebrate together.

Janie dipped her spoon into her oatmeal. She said nothing about her idea to Mrs. Hull.

But Janie had a plan.

CHAPTER 15

"And It Came to Pass"

Momma sat on the floor next to a fire and gazed at Janie. Momma's eyes looked just as warm as the fire itself. She moved over next to Janie and completely encircled her in her arms. Then Momma took both of Janie's hands and counted each finger out loud. She reached down and took Janie's bare feet and counted each toe out loud. It tickled when she did that, and Janie giggled. Momma began to laugh along with her. . . .

Janie woke up slowly, smiling. She lay in bed for a minute, letting the dream run through her mind. *Momma.* She'd been as real as if she'd been in the room.

It had been years since Janie had dreamed about her mother. These days she dreamed about Aunty Mil or the others left behind at Rubyhill. Once she had even dreamed about the white boy back near Tennessee—that he gave her a big basket full of live baby rabbits to play with, his blue eyes twinkling.

But this rare dream about Momma felt so real. Janie lay in bed awhile longer, half-asleep, letting the feel of Momma's almost-forgotten presence stay with her.

When she heard rustling in the room, Janie reluctantly got up. Lucy lay in the trundle bed next to the high-poster bed. She had asked to sleep upstairs with Janie and Aleta just for Christmas Eve, so that night Dr. Hull had carried Lucy up the stairs and placed her in the trundle bed. Aleta had tucked warm quilts around her, and Lucy drifted off to sleep right away.

Now Janie leaned over and looked down to find Lucy's eyes open. "Good morning, Lucy. How you doing?"

"Good morning, Janie," Lucy responded. "I'll be up in a minute." But Lucy's eyes closed again. Lucy never bounced out of bed these days. Janie knew she still needed time to gain back her strength.

Aleta rolled over. "Hey, you two—ready to get up?"

Janie and Aleta hopped onto the rugs, avoiding the cold wood floor as always, and they cleaned and dressed. Then Aleta sat at the foot of Lucy's bed. "Hey, little girl, want me to help you get up and dressed?"

Lucy opened her eyes, nodded, and sat up.

"I'll go downstairs and see if Maydean's come yet," said Janie. She bounded out of the room and down the stairs.

Twelve! Janie thought as she opened the door to the warm kitchen. *I am twelve years old today!* Momma's face from the dream flashed in her mind, and she felt a momentary twinge of sadness alongside her excitement.

Betsy set down the blue-speckled coffeepot and looked up. "Merry Christmas, Janie," she said.

Blue stood at the door with his heavy clothes on, drinking from a mug of coffee heavily laced with cream and sugar. "Mornin', Janie-bird. Merry Christmas, girl. And happy birthday, too!"

"Yes," Betsy beamed. "Happy birthday to you!" She paused and added, " 'Janie-bird?' "

It had been awhile since anyone had called Janie that, and it was bittersweet. "That's what Aunty Mil called me," she explained.

Betsy smiled. "Because you made a 'joyful noise,' yes?"

Janie grinned and nodded.

Blue set down his mug. "I'll be back 'fore long. Got to help Dr. Hull with the snow." He headed for the back door.

"Maydean's not here yet?" asked Janie.

"Not yet." Betsy opened the oven and pulled out hot biscuits, which she dumped onto a linen towel. Then she stirred applesauce on the stove and added cinnamon to it. "Hungry?"

"Yes, ma'am." Janie sat at one of the table places set with dishes and silverware. "Betsy, I been thinkin' on something."

Betsy picked up the applesauce pan and poured its contents into a heavy dish. "What's that?"

"I want to share my birthday with Lucy and Nathan."

Betsy kept her eyes on the hot items. "How do you mean?"

"Well, nobody from Rubyhill knows their birthday 'cept me. It's not right that I'm the only one gets a birthday. I don't know when Aleta and Blue were born, and I don't know that they care all that much. But I do know Nathan and Lucy were born in win- tertime just like me. I want to give them my birthday. We three can share it, can't we?"

Betsy stopped working and looked at Janie. "Why, I think that's a grand idea." She sat down across from Janie. "How do you want to do this?"

And plans were made.

That day, the Hulls, Betsy, and the Rubyhill Five did what Mrs. Hull had promised they'd do on Christmas morning. After breakfast, they gathered in the dining room, where a fire burned nicely. Mrs. Hull lit tall candles in the center of a fine mahogany table upon which sat a very large black Bible. Dr. Hull took a seat at the head of the table and invited the others to join him.

First Dr. Hull offered a short prayer of thanks. Then he opened to the second chapter of the Gospel of Luke and began to read, " 'And it came to pass. . . .' " The big Bible was passed around, and each person took his or her turn reading a few verses from the Christmas story.

The story unfolded of Mary and Joseph's difficult journey, the birth of baby Jesus, the shepherds, the angels—all of it very exciting to Janie. It wasn't easy for the young readers to pronounce all the words they came upon, but they did their best. Janie felt very special taking part in the reading.

As the reading went on, Janie marveled at how the very Son of God had been born in such a humble way, right in a barn among the animals. *Why, Aunty Mil's cabin would have been more comfortable than that,* thought Janie.

She wished Aunty Mil were right here so that Janie could read this exciting Christmas story to her. The dear old woman loved Jesus, but Janie wondered how much of this story—or any of the Bible—Aunty Mil really knew. Then the thought came to Janie: *Aunty Mil lives with Jesus. She knows all of this now.* It was a wonderful thing to consider.

When the reading was done, a comfortable silence settled over the group. The fire crackled, and candle flames waved gently in the house drafts as the meaning of the good words lingered.

Only one thing marred the reading of Luke this snowy Christmas morning.

Maydean had not come.

CHAPTER 16

Where's Maydean?

No doubt about it, Christmas dinner was the most delicious feast any of the Rubyhill Five had ever experienced in all their young lives.

Dinner was held at midday in the dining room, where the Bible reading had been. The long mahogany table was spread with a thick, lacy tablecloth, flowered china, and silverware Janie had not seen before. A vase of yew branches and holly graced the center. The table looked very handsome.

Janie was glad Betsy had taught them how to use silverware. None of the Rubyhill youths had ever held a fork before arriving at the Hull farm. They'd actually never even sat together around a table for meals before arriving here. Slaves did not have access to fancy silverware or table linens—or even dinner tables, for that matter. So table manners were taught kindly at the Hull kitchen school, right alongside reading and arithmetic.

After everyone was seated at the festive table, Dr. Hull offered grace. Then Betsy and Mrs. Hull served the meal. There was roast turkey, cornbread stuffing loaded with sausage and sage, potatoes and gravy, butternut squash, green beans cooked with bacon, side dishes of sweet pickles and succotash, and more flaky, golden biscuits than they could possibly finish. It came as no surprise that everyone was too full for dessert, so Mrs. Hull suggested they eat that later on.

Janie leaned back in her chair and stopped herself from fingering the outline of the pewter cross under her bodice. She felt so full she thought she would burst.

She thought about her wonderful day so far—the vivid dream about her mother, the morning Bible reading, the satisfying feast. In spite of it all, though, Janie found herself with one nagging worry.

Maydean still had not shown up.

Nobody had come up with any possible explanation for her absence, and this special holiday at the Hull farm was simply carrying on without her. Janie could not imagine Maydean intentionally missing that Bible reading on Christmas morning. And she certainly never missed meals at the Hull place, either—something Janie understood all too well. So where was Maydean?

Betsy stood and clapped her hands. "Everyone, we have a surprise for you!" Janie knew this had to do with birthdays.

But suddenly there was a knock on the front door. Betsy looked at the Hulls briefly, then hurried out to the foyer. When the door opened, a gust of wind came into the dining room. In the hallway, they heard Betsy cry out.

Dr. Hull rose quickly and put up his hand to indicate that they were to remain quiet. He hurried into the hallway. "Oh, child," they heard him say. "Come in, come in."

Maydean? Janie abandoned her new table manners, jumped up from the table, and ran to the hallway.

Maydean stood in the hallway, covered with snow. Janie could see that she had no coat or boots on under that snow—just pants, a man's shirt, a sweater, and what looked like slippers. Her hair hung wild, no longer braided, and it, too, was covered with snow.

When Janie stepped closer, she saw that Maydean's face was swollen. Then she saw that one side was covered in deep purple bruises. Maydean didn't even look like Maydean.

"What happened, child?" said Dr. Hull in a kind but tight voice. Betsy cried silent tears as she peeled the snow-covered sweater off Maydean and dropped it onto the rug.

"He was out all night, drunk," Maydean said simply.

"Thy grandfather?"

The girl nodded. "I got up and around this morning like usual. I was gonna come here soon as I could. He was there, drunker than I ever seen him. He gets mighty mean, so I tried to stay outta his way." Maydean paused and touched her head. "I had my braids still pinned up on my head, like you and me did 'em yesterday, Miss Betsy."

Betsy began rubbing Maydean's red hands and said nothing.

"Kept hittin' on my face," Maydean continued. "Then he pulled on my hair 'til all the braidin' was gone. I guess I'm lucky I still got any hair left." Maydean sighed and touched her bruised face. She winced. "I got away and run here."

"Janie, please get Mrs. Hull," said Betsy.

Janie turned and almost collided with Mrs. Hull, who was carrying a crocheted blanket from the front room. Mrs. Hull draped the blanket around the shoulders of the shivering Maydean and squeezed her tightly. "There, there. Thee is safe now," she heard Mrs. Hull say.

Aleta and Janie ran upstairs and gathered warm clothes for Maydean. As they hurried about, they heard Dr. Hull ask Maydean if she'd been hurt anywhere else. She had not, but she was terribly cold.

When the girls started back downstairs, they saw Dr. Hull pick the frozen girl up and carry her to the kitchen. Then he pulled Mrs. Hull into another room to talk to her, leaving Maydean in Betsy's care.

Janie and Aleta hurried into the kitchen where Maydean stood in front of the oven. Betsy began to peel the rest of her snow-packed clothing off. She wrapped Maydean in a big flannel blanket and rubbed the girl's arms and legs vigorously through that.

Betsy began toweling Maydean's hair, all the time chattering away. "We'll get that swelling down, and we'll get you into these warm clothes. I'll brush your hair out all nice, sweetie, and I'll braid it up for you again."

Maydean simply stood in silence, staring straight ahead. She looked wobbly to Janie.

Mrs. Hull bustled into the kitchen, a gentle smile on her face. "Maydean, child, thee shall stay here tonight. It's all arranged. Lucy goes back to her own room today, so thee can sleep in her bed upstairs."

Maydean turned to Mrs. Hull, her eyes wide and anxious.

Mrs. Hull seemed to understand. "Dr. Hull has decided to deliver Christmas food to thy grandfather, child. He and Blue are arranging this as we speak." She paused, then continued. "Alcohol is an evil thing, and it can overpower the goodness in any man. But the Lord has been known to break many a stubborn heart, so we shall pray for thy grandfather, Maydean. For now, thee shall stay here with us. Dr. Hull will not allow thee to be harmed again. And he will approach thy grandfather in peace."

Maydean's shoulders slumped and her eyes welled up with tears. Janie touched her friend's chapped hands. "You'll stay upstairs with Aleta and me, Maydean. You'll like it up there."

With that, Maydean sat down at the kitchen table and finally cried.

CHAPTER 17

A Happy Birthday

Dusk fell over the snowy fields of the Hull farm. In the warm, white farmhouse, dinner dishes had been washed and put away. Lucy and Mrs. Hull were taking naps in their rooms while Aleta finished tidying up the kitchen.

In the front room, Betsy turned on oil lamps for Nathan, Janie, and Maydean. The young redhead sat curled on a sofa. She was now clad in a warm flannel nightgown and robe, and she kept a heavy coverlet over her lap. It had taken a long time to warm Maydean up after her cold journey. Now all nice and snug with some hot food in her stomach, Maydean looked ready to go to sleep.

Nevertheless, Maydean's sleepy eyes followed the comings and goings of the others in the room. She seemed content to say nothing but to simply bask in the warm safety of the Hull home. She especially liked it when Nathan and Janie took turns reading aloud to her from the second chapter of Luke. They wanted her to hear the beautiful story in the Bible's own words while the day was still Christmas.

Aleta dashed into the front room. "They're back from your granddaddy's," she said to Maydean. "I ran out when I saw them come into the yard. Blue told me your granddaddy accepted the food from Dr. Hull and was even polite about it."

Maydean looked very relieved to hear this.

"That's not all," said Aleta. "Blue says Dr. Hull told your granddaddy straight out that his grandbaby's not safe, not while he's living with the bottle. Dr. Hull told him you'll stay here until your granddaddy's in his right mind again. Blue says the old man took it all right. Even thanked Dr. Hull!"

Maydean pulled the coverlet up around her neck and looked around the room. "I'm awful glad to be here," she said.

"And we're so very glad to have you with us," said Betsy. "Do you feel like having your hair brushed?"

Maydean nodded and turned so that Betsy could sit behind her on the sofa. Betsy pulled a brush out of her apron pocket and slowly, carefully ran it through Maydean's tangled mane. "We'll have you fixed up in no time," said Betsy.

Maydean leaned her cheek—the one without the bruises—against the back of the sofa. Before long, in spite of the hair-brushing, she fell asleep. Betsy continued brushing, then wove two thick braids, and laid them gently on Maydean's shoulders.

Betsy gestured for them all to follow her. "Let's heat up some cider in the kitchen," she whispered. Everyone but the sleeping Maydean trooped to the kitchen table.

Mrs. Hull was one step ahead of them. Up from her nap, she was laying out Christmas desserts on big platters. Nathan's eyes lit up, and he watched each movement with sharp interest. Nathan loved sweets.

Betsy pulled Janie aside. "We'll do what we planned over dessert."

Janie glanced back toward the front room. "Are you sure?"

Betsy squeezed Janie's hand. "You know what I think? I have a feeling Maydean would like the attention to be directed away from her for a while. What do you think?"

Janie grinned and nodded. "I sure do think she'd like something happy to happen."

Betsy grinned back. "I agree with you, Janie. So let us conspire to launch our plan over dessert."

Dr. Hull and Blue came in from the snow. Lucy rose from her nap and wandered into the kitchen. Finally Mrs. Hull said, "Let's take our dessert to the front room and join Maydean. She should not miss a moment more of this holiday."

Treats and hot drinks were put on trays and moved to the front room. Maydean woke up and blinked. When she saw the cookies and candies, she smiled broadly.

"Is everybody here?" Betsy asked. "Let's all have a seat. Janie has something she'd like to say."

The adults settled into chairs and the youngsters onto rugs. Janie stood up and cleared her throat.

"Today's my birthday. Today I am twelve years old."

"Happy birthday, young Janie!" called out Dr. Hull.

"Thank you, sir," Janie responded with a short, funny curtsy—thanks to Betsy's coaching—in his direction. "But what I want to say is this. It's no fun to be the only one with a birthday to celebrate. I want to share mine." She turned to Nathan and Lucy. "Will you two share my birthday with me? Not just today but from now on?"

Nathan's eyes lit up. He turned to his twin. "I say yes! How 'bout you, Lucy? What do you say?"

Lucy blinked and smiled. Then she nodded with more vigor than anyone had seen her have since before the fever.

"Lucy says yes, too," said Nathan. "Thanks, Janie!" He thought for a minute. "Does that mean you're our big sister now?"

"I'd like that," Janie said, suddenly feeling shy and happy.

"Maybe not so big, though," teased Dr. Hull. Everyone laughed.

Nobody noticed Betsy had left the room until she rounded the corner with a gigantic birthday cake. She had written each of their names on top with buttercream frosting. And of course, each of them could read it. The room broke into applause.

"Well," said Mrs. Hull, clapping her hands, "isn't this wonderful? And all of it on the birthday of our Lord Jesus!" She turned to Nathan and Lucy. "This is a thrilling moment for both of thee. Thy family has increased today."

Mrs. Hull turned to Janie. "And thee has chosen to share what thee has with a glad heart. May our Lord bless thee, precious child."

Janie beamed. Dr. Hull stood and prayed over the group. When he finished, Lucy stood and came over to Janie. She hugged her.

That was a very nice gesture. But the best thing to Janie was that this was the most energetic movement Lucy had made in weeks.

Little Lucy was most certainly on the mend on this, her new official birthday.

DuPont Acres, Kentucky

Even in the middle of Kentucky, it snowed this Christmas Day. Anna made dinner for Mr. DuPont and all his hired hands. Then she retired to the room over the stable where she lived with George.

Anna wrapped her arms around her knees while she waited for George to finish feeding the horses. She had one thought on her mind. Today, like every Christmas, was her baby's birthday.

How many more Christmas Days must she wait to see her child again?

CHAPTER 18

Indiana Spring

Time passed quickly while the Rubyhill Five wintered at the Hull farm. It was a cold and snowy winter, more so than usual. But before long, the snow thawed and did not return.

Janie found that she loved the feel and smell of spring in Indiana. While spring was a vibrant time in Georgia, there was something about having weathered the cold and the snow that made an Indiana spring particularly beautiful.

It started with a sweetness in the air. Rain became warmer. Daffodils and tulips shot up next. Then came the fragrant lilacs and lilies of the valley, and soon just about everything was in blossom. Best of all, Janie was allowed to watch the births of lambs and calves. There was new life everywhere.

In the big farmhouse, another bed had been moved into the girls' room upstairs. Now Aleta, Lucy, Janie, and Maydean all shared the big bedroom. Betsy had a small room to herself at the end of the upstairs hall. Janie felt as if she had lots of sisters, and she liked the feeling.

All of the youths on the Hull farm had gained much-needed weight and strength over the winter, and they all looked good and healthy. Good nutrition and lifestyle added to the eagerness of all the kitchen-table students to learn everything they could. Mrs.

Hull and Betsy continued to teach their students as much as they could handle and then pushed them to learn even more.

By spring, everyone could read and write fluently. They could perform any math task asked of them. They could write and deliver short speeches on any number of topics, their manners were beyond acceptable, and the Bible was becoming a familiar friend.

Janie never ceased to be amazed at how Maydean blossomed after moving in with the Hulls. She was turning into a bright and beautiful young woman. Betsy had taken the girl under her wing and taught her how to groom and dress herself and to polish the rough edges of her speech and manners.

Now Maydean wore her braids pinned up like Betsy's. Janie liked the way it looked and began to do the same. She liked to pin her braids in a spiral at the back of her head.

It thrilled everybody that Maydean was studying already to apply for teachers' college. She also practiced writing letters so that she could stay in touch with Betsy next year when Betsy moved to Detroit.

Janie was glad about the letter-writing in particular. She and Maydean planned to write each other many letters. Janie knew that the Rubyhill Five would be moving on soon.

There was no question as to whether or not all five Rubyhill youths would continue traveling north, even though it would be dreadfully hard to leave the Hull farm. But they were all committed to starting a new life in Chicago. The only question was when.

One morning in early April, Janie could hardly wait to finish her breakfast of sausage and biscuits with jam. Dr. Hull had told her only half an hour earlier that a foal would be born of her favorite mare that morning, and Janie didn't want to miss this for anything. She ate so fast she didn't even talk to Lucy and Nathan, who joined her at the table. Then Blue came to breakfast.

"Hey, y'all," said Blue pouring himself a cup of coffee. "It's one fine day outside."

"I'm a little late getting out there," said Nathan. "You already do your chores?"

Blue nodded and sat down. He stirred milk and sugar into his coffee, then looked around the table. "Where's Aleta?"

"Don't you usually know?" teased Janie.

Blue grinned and took a sip of coffee. Then he cleared his throat. "Look, Janie, Nathan, Lucy. . ." He paused. "Aleta and I have been talking. Let me just come out and say that I know we're having a good life here. But it's spring. That means it's time for us to get moving again."

Janie stopped eating. Of course she always knew the day would come when she would have to leave these people she'd come to know and love. She felt sick to her stomach.

Nathan and Lucy were quiet, too. Blue waited. Then he said, "Anyone want to say anything?"

Nobody said a word.

"I'm thinking we could leave in a few days," Blue went on. "What do you think about that?"

"I–I guess that would be fine," stammered Nathan. Lucy's dark eyes grew wide, but she said nothing.

Finally, Janie spoke. "I don't want to leave yet, Blue."

Blue nodded. "I kinda thought you might say that. But, Janie-bird, but you might never want to leave if we don't get going fairly soon. You didn't want to leave Rubyhill, either, remember?"

Janie nodded. "How long you think we'll have to be on the road?" she asked. The thought of leaving the comforts of the Hull house was not a pleasant one.

Blue cocked his head and thought. "Oh, about a couple weeks, depending on how things go. Think you can do it?"

Janie looked at the tablecloth. "I don't know. I guess so."

Blue reached over and touched Janie's hand. "Hey, you. We're family, you know. We're all together in this. God's been good to us, leading us here to the Hulls. They've prepared us for near about everything. But I don't think we're meant to stay here forever. Do you?"

The days here at the Hull farm had been so full that Janie hadn't really thought about the future. But deep down inside, she had to agree. Their destination remained Chicago.

Janie looked at Blue, then at Nathan and Lucy. "I'd like it if we could stay until after Easter. That's two weeks more."

"Then we will," said Blue.

DuPont Acres, Kentucky

Anna brought the subject up first. They had just finished breakfast in their room over the stable. "When we headed for Chicago, George?"

George stopped cleaning his boots and looked at his wife, but he didn't answer. Instead, he went back to cleaning his boots.

"We got enough cash now," Anna said.

George looked up at her, then back down. "Well, sugar, the thing is, I promised DuPont I'd stay through foaling."

Anna stared at George. "We got enough cash now," she said

again, as if he hadn't heard her.

"I promised him I'd stay through foaling," George repeated softly.

Anna's anger flared up, fast. "What you talking about?"

George answered his wife calmly and slowly. "I should've talked to you about it first, Anna. But I gave the man my word."

"You gave him your word?" Anna stood up. "And what about me, George? What about what you promised me, that we'd find our girl? What about that? What's your word worth there?"

George stopped working and looked at the floor.

Anna marched to the window and stood with her back to her husband until he left for work.

Nothing more was said about Chicago again for weeks.

CHAPTER 19

Chicago

Chicago sure is windy, thought Janie.

It was the middle of May, and the Rubyhill Five found themselves right in the center of the largest city they'd ever seen. Indiana seemed like a long time ago. Now instead of living with the Hulls, Betsy, and Maydean, the youths were encountering hundreds of strangers—black, white, Chinese, Indian, Mediterranean, rich, poor, and even in between. When the five of them first arrived in the city, they found it so curious and fascinating that they simply wandered the streets for two hours.

People hurried up and down the first sidewalks the Georgian friends had ever walked on. The many shopwindows showed merchandise that the young people had never dreamed of buying. Vendors cooked and sold food right on the street, and the smoky smells beckoned the Rubyhill Five on every block. The force from all those people was so strong that Janie felt she could reach out and touch it.

Then there was the Great Lake Michigan, its shores right in the city. What a powerful body of water, deep blue and full of whitecaps. Alongside the docks, dozens of fishermen displayed their wares. In the distance, large ships sailed on the lake's long horizon. To Janie, they looked like strange, breathing creatures crawling along.

Here in Chicago, Janie at first battled instant fear. She had never been around so many people in her life—noisy ones at that. And she had never seen a body of water bigger than a wide part of the Ohio River. This water seemed to go on forever. She could not even see the other side of the lake.

Blue and Nathan were thrilled at seeing the city and the huge lake with its ships. Aleta praised the fashions the women wore. Even Lucy chattered excitedly about the fresh fish they'd fry. Janie simply stared at everything and made certain to stick close by the others.

The five young people had traveled through most of Indiana on foot. But several miles south of the outskirts of Chicago, they had decided to use some of their money and finish this journey by train. Thankfully, they'd never before dipped into that cash they'd found so long ago at Rubyhill. Now was the time.

So there was another first for the Rubyhill Five. They'd never boarded a train before. Fortunately, one of their lessons at the Hull kitchen-table school had been how to read train schedules. Mrs. Hull had also given them practice in using money and figuring change as part of their math lessons. Dr. Hull stepped in toward the end of their stay to teach them how to read maps and street plans.

The friends remained ever grateful for the help they had received in so many ways at the kind hands of Dr. and Mrs. Hull and Betsy. Never could the Rubyhill Five have entered this cosmopolitan city with confidence had they not wintered with the Hulls, receiving nourishment, education, and practical skills the entire time.

Back in Indiana, Dr. Hull had been positive and helpful about the upcoming journey to Chicago. He told them that as country people, they might find the city challenging at first, but there was no reason to fear the people there. He confirmed what had been rumored in Georgia, that a black person could live nearly as well as a white person in Chicago.

Dr. Hull had even written down the address of what he called a *benevolent society*—a place of goodwill that had helped runaway slaves get established in Chicago. Even though slavery was now abolished, the director of the society, a Mr. Solomon, would happily help them find lodging and possibly work.

The other exciting thing Dr. Hull wrote down was the name and address of a church pastored by a black minister, a Reverend Silas. This man had wintered at the Hull farm many years ago during his own escape from slavery. He had gone on to attend seminary and become a minister. Now he was pastor of a substantial Chicago church. "Go to that church straightaway," Dr. Hull told them. "Reverend Silas will help thee, as well. And it is a fine church community that will help thee in thy spiritual walk."

After allowing themselves time to gawk at the exciting things Chicago had to offer, the five young people circled back to the train depot so that they could follow Dr. Hull's written directions to the benevolent society. They headed down the sidewalk as directed by their notes.

Janie was grateful that these sidewalks kept dangerous, fast-moving horses and wagons at bay. While some of Chicago's streets were made of brick, many streets were still dirt and, at this time of year, muddy. Walking on the sidewalks was not only safer, but it also helped keep their clothes clean. The Georgian youths did not want to appear to be country bumpkins, and staying neat and clean was important.

It was an amazing thing to stand in the heart of the great city of Chicago, but it was even more amazing to have the ability to read. There were so many signs to read. Janie did not remember seeing signs with words in the South. Of course, she had never been to a southern city, but she figured maybe they had had signs. In the Georgia countryside, she'd heard there were crossroads markers, but those had been taken down during the war to confuse the Yankee soldiers. Janie had never seen them, anyway. She'd never left the plantation back then, and in their journey north, they had stayed off main roads.

So in Chicago, while the wind whipped down the sidewalks with a vengeance, Lucy and Janie read the shop signs aloud to each other, rolling new words and names on their tongues. JANSSEN'S BAKERY. CITY INSURANCE. CORNER BUTCHER. LIVERY. MRS. MILLER'S ALTERATIONS.

Finally, Blue called out, "Here's the street! Dr. Hull said the building numbers go up and down in order, so let's figure out which way to go for number 32."

"There!" called Nathan, pointing west. "The numbers go up that way."

They turned down the street until Blue halted in front of a handsome, four-story, brick building. He looked once more at his notes, then nodded. They all piled inside to a hallway where there was no wind.

People hurried in and out the door, barely taking notice of the youths. Clearly, people in this city were used to seeing strangers, and it looked to Janie like white folks and black folks seemed to mix and get along all right together.

"See if you can find Mr. Solomon's name on these doors,"

said Aleta. They moved slowly up the hall until Janie spied the man's name.

Inside the greeting area of Mr. Solomon's office, the atmosphere was homey. A fire burned low in a huge wall fireplace that was big enough so that Janie, Lucy, and Nathan could have fit inside it. They all stood in front of the fire.

"May I help you?" said a woman's voice behind them.

The five young people whirled around. A white woman had risen from behind a desk. She was tall, and her hair was gray. She wore tiny eyeglasses, and she gave what Janie sensed was a warm and genuine smile.

"Excuse us," said Aleta. "You have a nice fire. . . ." She stopped. An awkward silence followed as they stood at the fireplace.

The tall white woman nodded. "Enjoy it as long as you like."

Aleta spoke again. "We're here to meet Mr. Solomon."

The white woman nodded. "Do you have an appointment?"

"No, ma'am," said Aleta.

"Did anyone in particular send you?"

"Yes," said Aleta, "Dr. Otto Hull in Indiana."

"Ah, yes. You wintered there?"

All five nodded.

The woman continued. "A good man, Dr. Hull. How is he? And Mrs. Hull, is she well?"

None of the five from Rubyhill were used to talking to strange white people, even after living with the Hulls. To engage in casual conversation with white strangers was very new to them.

But Aleta carried the day, telling the woman any news she could think of regarding the Hulls. "And we have a letter of introduction from Dr. Hull," she finished.

"Excellent," said the white woman. "Let me take it to Mr. Solomon."

Aleta relinquished the letter to the tall woman, who said, "Please have a seat."

Janie realized that had they not spent time with the Hulls, they never could have approached this organization of white people, strangers all. But the Rubyhill Five had learned enough social graces to do just fine. Aleta had just shown them how it was done.

The five young people sat down on a row of straight chairs against the wall. As they waited, Janie thought about their last day at the Hull farm. How difficult it had been to say good-bye. Mrs. Hull had held her close and promised her they'd see one another again, and if not on earth, they'd meet in heaven. "Thee knows there will come a time of no good-byes, yes, child?"

Dr. Hull's face would have been unreadable had his eyes not been shining in an odd manner. Janie wondered if those were a strong man's tears. He hugged each of them tightly. "We thank God for sending thee to us, and we shall dearly miss thee all," was all he said.

Betsy cried openly as they readied their things on the last day. She packed lots of tasty carrying food for the group, and once they were on the road, they saw that she'd also wrapped and packed a Bible in with the food. It was a much-welcomed surprise, just as they knew Betsy intended it to be.

Maydean kept a stiff upper lip that last day, but her eyes betrayed her. Janie knew the bedroom would be especially lonely for Maydean once the girls left. She decided Maydean should have the pewter cross.

Before leaving that day, Janie draped the silver chain around her friend's neck without comment. Maydean clutched the cross in her hand. "Thank you, my friend," she whispered. She turned the cross over and read the inscription again, then looked up. "Make that joyful noise, Janie, no matter what. And write to me."

Janie had simply nodded, too full of emotion to speak.

On the day the Rubyhill Five started their last leg of the journey north, nobody stood at the gate and sang to them. The Quakers were not singers like those at Rubyhill. Just the same, the power of their love and prayers sustained the young people all the way to Chicago.

The tall woman's voice interrupted Janie's thoughts. "Mr. Solomon will see you now."

CHAPTER 20

New Places, New Faces

Mr. Solomon was a kind man and every bit as helpful as Dr. Hull had said he would be. Soon enough, the Rubyhill Five found themselves moving into a clean and respectable boardinghouse.

The three-story, solid-brick house sat in a neighborhood of mostly black and immigrant families. The boardinghouse was owned and run by Mrs. Babbs, a big woman with a big heart. The girls shared a room on the women's second floor, and Nathan and Blue shared a room on the men's third floor. They took meals with the other boarders in a long dining room on the first floor.

All five found jobs right away. Janie and Lucy worked in restaurant kitchens, and Aleta sewed for a tailor. Blue and Nathan both loaded cargo at the docks.

There were no laws to make children attend school in those days. There also were no laws against hiring children. Some businesses even preferred hiring children because they could pay them less. The Rubyhill Five did not know this. They only knew that as former slaves, they'd never earned money before at all, so to be paid for one's labor truly felt like a step up.

Other than the Yankee cash from Rubyhill, cash on hand was still a new thing for the Georgia youths. Each earned enough money to pay room and board and have a little left over.

Fortunately Mrs. Hull had drilled them on how to handle money. She also had taught them to first give away ten cents of every dollar. This was a biblical habit called *tithing*, she informed them. Most people would give that tithed money to a church, but Janie also liked to look for people in need on the street and give to them, as well.

As soon as Janie could afford it, she bought her own Bible; the rest of her earnings she saved. Janie took the worn piece of fabric from Aunty Mil's chair and stitched it into a drawstring purse, and that was where she kept her savings. She stuffed the purse deep into her pinafore pocket and carried it all the time.

Janie realized that Dr. Hull had been right about another thing. Living in the city was a lot different from living in the country. After the initial thrill of Chicago wore off, Janie found she had some adjustments to make. For her, city life was jarring—noisy, dirty, and laced with bad smells. Its intensity was a shock to her country-girl nature every single day. And the Chicago summer was horribly hot and muggy with no relief.

Eventually, however, Janie learned to find what she loved in the city. She missed the farm animals, but she got to know the slow-moving milk-wagon horses, the alley cats begging for scraps, and the many birds. Janie liked to watch and feed pigeons, cardinals, and sparrows, all flying free above the clamor and congestion of the city.

The other part of nature Janie soon learned to love was Lake Michigan, and she came to appreciate living beside such a rare and grand force of nature. She found the crashing waves exhilarating, the sound of the foghorns comforting, and the flocks of screaming seagulls great fun. In that first hot Chicago summer, the Rubyhill youths learned that spending evenings at the lake could cool them down for sleeping. Sometimes on Sundays, very early, Janie went to the lakeshore alone to think and pray.

Chicago offered other things Janie had never thought about before. Access to libraries where she could read and borrow books made her feel incredibly wealthy. Free concerts of music of all kinds cropped up in parks all over the city. She heard public lectures and speeches on all kinds of topics and issues. She did not want to spend the money to attend the theater, but once she and the twins splurged and attended a circus. Nathan talked for a while about finding work there until he learned that the circus people stayed on the road all the time. "I'm done with that kind of life," he said.

Unfortunately, Janie also observed that even though all kinds of people lived and worked together on these streets, Chicago did have whites who treated black people as inferior. And some blacks treated the immigrants as inferior. It seemed the many different kinds of people here did not necessarily like one another, Janie decided. They simply tolerated the situation of living together.

Nevertheless, the Georgian youths did sense a sure and certain freedom they would never have had back home, and they enjoyed every moment of it. Black people walked free and proud in Chicago. Black neighborhoods packed with black-owned businesses thrived. Chicagoans were not always warm, but they were helpful, and they respected hard work.

Best of all, Janie and her friends attended a big, beautiful church. Dr. Hull's friend Reverend Silas was pastor of a large AME church, which stood for the African Methodist Episcopal denomination. For Janie, who had no church background other than the quiet Quaker meetings in Indiana and the services in the pine groves back at Rubyhill, the reverend's church services were dramatic and thrilling. Especially the music.

To Janie, music at Reverend Silas's church was a little like the fieldworkers' music back home, only this was faster, more upbeat, and fuller of sound. There were women singers who could make the hair stand up on Janie's neck, they were that powerful. Janie loved singing with them, and she was grateful she could read the words in the hymnal. Some members played musical instruments—piano, drums, trumpets, and tambourines—during church. Reverend Silas pointed out that young David of the Old Testament was their musical example in this regard.

Chicago women, Janie observed, wore hats and other head coverings when out and about, and this appealed to young Janie. At age twelve going on thirteen, she felt like she was almost a woman herself. One day, she pulled Aunty Mil's faded yellow head scarf out from under her pillow and inhaled the comforting but fading scent of Aunty Mil's hair one more time. Then Janie tied the head scarf over her own pinned-up braids. She ran downstairs to look at herself in the hall mirror. She may still be small, but she looked grown-up. Janie wore the head scarf from then on.

So the days in Chicago were full and rich. Janie wrote long letters to Maydean, enclosing shorter ones to be delivered to the Hulls and to Betsy. She detailed every move the Rubyhill Five made in their new life and every decision as well. In August, Janie was elected to write to the Hull farm about the biggest news of all.

Blue and Aleta were getting married.

Train Station, Chicago

The Chicago-bound train huffed slowly into the station. George took his wife's hand, and the two of them stood with their faces in the open window of their passenger car. True to his word, George had put Anna and himself on a train for the journey from Kentucky to Chicago. There would be no more walking for his wife on this trip.

Neither of them had ever been in a city like Chicago before. George had finally told Anna how he'd spent his seven long years away from her. The chain gang that bought him at Shannon Oaks had marched him all the way to the hot Louisiana city of New Orleans, where he spent many painful years working as a slave. It had been a horrible life.

It had been hard for Anna to hear about it, but it drew them closer when George finally shared his story with her. Living as a slave in New Orleans was nothing like riding into the great city of Chicago as a free man. Praise the Lord, how far He had brought them!

George pulled Anna close to him. "I am so sorry I made you wait for this trip, sugar. You should never have to wait for anything again."

Anna laid her head on her husband's shoulder. The fight of last spring was over, forgiven and forgotten. "We'll find her, George," she said. "We're so close I can feel it."

The train rolled to a stop.

Chapter 21

Good News

Janie sat with Mrs. Babbs at the breakfast table and sipped her morning tea. It was early Sunday morning, and the other boarders were still sleeping. Fortunately, Mrs. Babbs, like Janie, was an early riser, so the two of them often enjoyed morning tea together.

"Miss Janie," said Mrs. Babbs, "I have been meaning to tell you about an experience I believe you might enjoy."

Janie loved listening to Mrs. Babbs speak. She had a deep melodious voice and spoke formally to everyone. It was part of her unique warmth and charm.

"Yes, Mrs. Babbs?" Janie carefully set her cup in its saucer, then folded her hands in her lap as Mrs. Hull had taught her.

"A great speaker is coming to our fair city. On Saturday next, she will speak at the Temperance Hall."

"She?" said Janie. Even in Chicago, Janie had not heard of such a thing as a woman delivering a public speech. Janie didn't really count church testimonies in that category.

"Yes, dear, *she*. Her name is Sojourner Truth, and she is a powerful speaker. I have heard her before."

"Sojourner," Janie repeated. "What a beautiful name."

"She chose her name, Miss Janie. She had a slave's name, and she changed it to reflect her true mission in this world. She says she is but a sojourner through life, put into this world to speak only truth. She was an abolitionist prior to the war, and now she speaks of the rights of women."

Unfortunately Janie would have to miss this event. "I'm afraid I won't be able to attend, Mrs. Babbs. The restaurant is very strict about missing work on Saturdays."

Mrs. Babbs nodded sympathetically.

"But I'm glad you brought this up, Mrs. Babbs," Janie continued. "It's her name that impresses me. It makes me think that maybe I could change my own name."

"Yes, Miss Janie, you could. Sojourner Truth certainly did."

Janie thought back to when she and the others had filled out paperwork at Mr. Solomon's place that first day in Chicago. None of them knew their last names. If any of them had one, they'd never heard it. Janie had felt a sense of shame about this for the first time. It was one more indignity from having been slaves.

That day, the Rubyhill Five had excused themselves for a moment in Mr. Solomon's office. They had huddled in the hall and came to the decision to borrow the Hull name for the time being. Janie still called herself Janie Hull.

Mrs. Babbs brought Janie back to the present. "If I may be so bold as to ask, Miss Janie, what might you change your name to, if you were so inclined? And would you care for more tea?"

"No, thank you, Mrs. Babbs." Janie paused. "My given name was Georgeanna, but I've always been called Janie. As much as I like Georgeanna—those are my parents' first names—I'm used to being called Janie." She stirred her remaining tea thoughtfully. "You know, Mrs. Babbs, my last name isn't really Hull, either. Most of us here from Georgia aren't even blood family. We all took our last name from the Quakers we wintered with."

Before Mrs. Babbs could respond, they heard tromping down the stairs. Blue and Nathan appeared in the doorway. Blue snapped to attention and gave a slight bow to Mrs. Babbs, who always loved such a show of courtesy. Nathan immediately followed suit.

"Sit down, gentlemen," Mrs. Babbs cooed. "Will you both be wanting coffee this morning?"

"Yes, ma'am, that would be fine," Blue said in a charming tone. Nathan nodded, and they both sat.

When Mrs. Babbs rose and went to the kitchen, Blue turned to Janie. "Good morning, Janie-bird."

"That's it!" said Janie.

"What's what?" said Blue.

"That will be my new name. I mean, Bird will be my last name. Janie Bird. It will always remind me of Aunty Mil."

"I like that," Nathan said.

"You thinking on changing your name, Janie?" asked Blue. "Why don't you go back to Georgeanna?"

Mrs. Babbs moved into the dining room with coffee. She'd caught the tail end of the conversation. "If I may say," she said, "you might wish to use the name Georgeanna as your middle name."

"That's a whole lotta names," Nathan observed.

"But very proper," Mrs. Babbs assured them. "I am not sure how it is done in the South, but in Chicago, we do tend to give three names to newborns."

"Janie Georgeanna Bird," said Janie. It sounded pretty to her, like music. "I like that, Mrs. Babbs. Thank you. That will be my new name from this day on."

Blue grinned. "That's my girl. Good for you." He spooned sugar into his coffee and stirred it. Then Blue shared something he had never mentioned before. "I sometimes think about changing my name, too. Blue sounds like a slave name to me."

Nobody responded. Blue continued.

"My momma said I was named for my daddy, and I know my daddy was named for the color of his skin. They said he was 'blue-black.' "

Janie shuddered. Blue had beautiful coal-black skin. Apparently because of that, he had been named the same way people would name a horse—according to color. It was another shameful legacy from slavery.

"But you know," said Blue, "Aleta fell in love with me as Blue. And she and I think a lot of Dr. and Mrs. Hull—as if they were our own parents—so we might want to keep their name."

"You could give yourself a middle name," suggested Janie.

Blue considered that. "I could. I'll talk to Aleta about it. I can't say as I care much, but when we have children some day, it might matter then."

The table fell silent. Then the other boarders appeared for breakfast, and the subject was dropped.

Later at church, Reverend Silas announced the engagement of Blue and Aleta. The reverend congratulated the young couple from the pulpit and then surprised them by saying, "We are going to have a full worship service for these young people on their wedding day. It will be held on a Sunday morning and followed by the kind of feast this church knows how to fix."

The people of the congregation chuckled. Their church suppers were impressive indeed.

Reverend Silas looked directly at Blue and Aleta. "I am authorized by the state of Illinois to marry you legally, and I will do so with great joy. On that day, Blue and Aleta, you will be married in the eyes of God and in the eyes of the law."

Janie felt a shiver of excitement for her friends. Back in Georgia, when a slave had married, there was no church or law involved. Slaves had to ask permission to marry from their masters. If they were given approval—and there was no guarantee they would receive it—they followed a short ritual called *jumping the broom.*

In the ritual, the couple laid a straw broom on the ground, held hands, and jumped over it together. Then the couple was considered married. No minister, no paperwork. Freedom had not yet changed this ritual at Rubyhill. A black couple would still jump the broom to marry.

Janie looked over at Aleta and Blue. Their eyes were wide with wonder. This ceremony would be a lot stronger and more binding than merely jumping the broom. When they married, it would be a union approved by both God and the community, and nothing could tear them apart.

Nobody would ever be able to do to Blue and Aleta what had been done to Janie's parents.

Elsewhere in Chicago

George and Anna had a plan. They had saved enough money so that they did not need to find paying work right away in Chicago. Instead, they intended to spend all of their time and energy seeking out Janie's whereabouts.

Old Joe back at Rubyhill had suggested they try black-member churches and societies that helped people in need. He remembered those places from being in Chicago before the war, but he had no names or addresses for the couple.

It was of no consequence. George and Anna had worked hard to get north, and they would work hard now to find their daughter.

They started with the churches.

CHAPTER 22

A Wedding Day

Blue and Aleta's wedding fell on a sunny day in late September. One full year had passed since the day the five youths left Rubyhill. Whenever Janie thought about how much had happened that year, it made her head spin.

The week before the wedding, a handsome travel trunk arrived by train from the Hull farm. Inside were gifts for everyone, and there were exceptionally generous gifts for the happy couple.

A letter enclosed from Mrs. Hull explained that she and Betsy had seen this engagement coming a long time ago. Many weeks before they received Janie's letter with the actual news, the two Indiana women had begun to stitch a coverlet for the couple. That was finished and folded in the trunk alongside a new family Bible.

The wedding took place in the sanctuary of the AME church on a Sunday morning. True to his word, Reverend Silas conducted a beautiful worship service complete with lots of soul-stirring music, and he worked wedding vows into it all.

Janie, sitting with Nathan and Lucy in the front pew, was so happy she thought she'd burst. Aleta had never looked more beautiful, and Blue had never looked more handsome. Aleta wore a lovely deep blue dress she had sewn, and she carried a bouquet of colorful gladiolus from Mrs. Babbs's backyard. Janie wished the other former slaves from Rubyhill could be here to see this.

Janie's front pew seat was closest to the wall. She casually craned her neck to see who was in attendance behind her. There sat the choir ladies. Mrs. Babbs and some of the boarders were there. The Italian tailor who employed Aleta had come with his wife. Mr. Solomon attended, too.

The service started early and lasted a long time. When the wedding vows were finished, Reverend Silas raised his hand to pronounce Blue and Aleta as husband and wife. Janie heard a creak in the back of the sanctuary as the double doors to the entrance opened. She turned to see who had arrived so late.

A well-dressed man and woman stepped inside and looked around for a seat. Janie had never seen them in church before, and it didn't look like they realized a wedding was in process. Reverend Silas nodded at them and continued with his pronouncement, followed by a blessing. "Let us pray," he said then, and heads bowed.

But not Janie's. She couldn't take her eyes off the new couple who remained standing for the prayer. The woman's hand lay on the man's arm, and she kept it there as he removed his hat and bowed his head.

Janie took in their cinnamon skin and fine clothing. The way the woman cocked her head looked oddly familiar. Then for some reason, the woman raised her head and looked straight at Janie, showing her deep brown eyes.

When Reverend Silas said, "Amen," the congregation repeated the word and raised their heads. The pastor started to invite people to the wedding feast in the back room, but he stopped.

Little Janie Georgeanna Bird in the yellow head scarf was literally running down the church aisle to the back of the sanctuary. And Janie didn't care who was looking or even where she was. She knew who those people in the back were.

Momma had found her. And Poppa, too.

It took some time for everyone to calm down after the initial excitement of the reunion of George, Anna, and Janie. Once Reverend Silas understood what was going on, he announced to everyone that today the lost had been found. Good preacher that he was, he also took this opportunity to remind them that Christ had performed His first miracle at a wedding.

But Janie wasn't really listening to Reverend Silas. Momma was holding her so tightly, Janie didn't think she'd ever breathe again. But she stayed put. Momma's arms around her felt so good, just like that dream on Christmas morning.

Janie peeked up at her tall father. She could see that she looked a lot like him. After standing in shock for a moment, he wrapped his arms around both his wife and daughter and openly sobbed.

At that point, the church people wept, too. Even formal Mrs. Babbs pressed her starched handkerchief to her eyes.

Emotion traveled over the room like a wave for the next several minutes. When it finally had settled down, Momma released her tight hold on Janie but continued to hold her hand. Janie pulled her parents around the room and introduced them to all her friends, old and new.

After introductions were made and eyes wiped, the newlywed Blue raised his hand for attention. "I want to say something to all of you. Aleta and I appreciate this wedding day so much. We are husband and wife now in a way we never could have been back in Georgia."

Blue turned to Janie's father. "I am a happy bridegroom today, sir," he said, "and I have an idea. If you and your wife only jumped the broom to get married way back when, why don't you make this *your* true wedding day, too?"

Reverend Silas's eyes brightened. "What a spectacular idea, Blue." He faced George and Anna. "May I offer to conduct the ceremony that makes you married in the eyes of God and in the eyes of the law?"

George and Anna looked at Janie, then at each other. "Yes," they each said at the very same time. And they both laughed.

Another wedding was held at the AME church that day. Janie's family was together at last.